The Shadow
of Old London Town

AN EYEFUL
OF THE TOWER

Written and illustrated by
Loykey & Lillybit

Loykey & Lillybit

This edition first published 2021 by
Loykey & Lillybit

A CIP record for this book
is available from the British Library

ISBN 978-0-9562333-6-3

Printed in Great Britain by
Biddles Books Limited, King's Lynn, Norfolk

INTRODUCTION

Au revoir New York City
Bonjour Paris
Cobweb Joe takes a bow
And say to Matt and Molly chow
Now another new City
No Cobweb Joe what a pity
The Eiffel Tower looks so grand
Looking over Disneyland
Many black taxis instead of yellow
Parlez-vous anglais says a young fellow
Codes and clues they will shout
Without a shadow of a doubt
TAP, TAP, TAP ......

CHAPTERS

1.

PARLEZ-VOUS ANGLAIS

2.

BOOK OF HOURS

3.

KISS KISS

4.

LUXOR WILL TAKE YOU HIGH

5.

TASTE OF U.S.A.

6.

BELLS WILL RING

7.

ON YOUR BIKE BOYS

CHAPTERS

8.

NAPOLEON'S RETURN

9.

THE LOUVRE DOORS WILL LET YOU IN

10.

UP UP AND AWAY

11.

THE SHADOW OF THE PAST

12.

A WINTER WONDERLAND

13.

A GHOSTLY ENDING

PARIS,
FRANCE

CHAPTER 1

PARLEZ-VOUS ANGLAIS?

Matt and Molly are 10 years of age and, once again, on their way to experiencing a new way of life in Paris.

The journey by plane is approximately seven hours, from New York City to Charles de Gaulle Airport.

It was the biggest plane they had ever been on, and they all had seats next to each other. Dad said, "Nearly there."

Matt replied, "Now are you going to tell us where we shall be living, or is it still a secret?"

Molly said, "Mum, please tell him to share the secret."

"OK, Paris," replied Dad.

Molly whispered to Matt, "Great! We already know that."

Matt said, "Just give us a clue."

Dad took a deep breath and said, "Well, it would be insane to stay there! Now that is all I am telling you."

Matt and Molly drifted off to sleep, both thinking of the clue. Matt was also wondering how their friend *The Shadow* was getting on, stuck down in the hold. Thank goodness he was not making an entrance - a ghost on a plane would not go down too well. Bertie was fast asleep, and not a peep.

The twins were finally woken with the Captain's voice announcing the weather conditions in Paris. "It is cold and wet, without a shadow of doubt, so umbrellas at the ready."

Matt and Molly laughed at his statement, and everybody thought they were mad being happy about the horrible, wet day.

The plane landed and, after a long wait getting through Customs, Dad said, "Come on, there is a taxi." Standing in the bay was a policeman, waiting to open the cab door for them.

Dad said, "Merci beaucoup, monsieur."

In they all piled with all their cases safely in the boot, ready to greet their new home.

The taxi driver started the conversation and Mum answered, as she was fluent in French. He asked her if she could hear a *TAP, TAP, TAP* as he thought something was in the boot! He stopped the taxi, and the noise stopped, too.

Matt and Molly knew exactly what the noise was, which meant *The Shadow* was now out of the large trunk-case.

After twenty minutes, they arrived at their destination. There in front of them was their new home. A row of five-storey town houses and, right at the end, stood the Eiffel Tower.

The little Frenchman unloaded their bags onto the pavement and, in broken English, pointed out that one of the cases was open.

Dad zipped up the case and said to Matt, "Well, you didn't make a good job of that one, son; thank goodness nothing is missing!"

Molly just grinned.

"Sorry Dad," replied Matt, at the same time thinking, where was *The Shadow*?

Dad took out his wallet and paid the driver with euros. That was another thing that Matt and Molly were going to have to get used to, as they had been paying in dollars and cents.

Dad said, "Well kids, this is our home for the next year - 13 Avenue Silvestre de Sacy."

Mum said, "I think we will just refer to it as Number 13, agreed?"

Matt replied, "I'm going to call it Stallone!"

Dad scratched his head and said, "Sorry?"

Matt replied, "Sylvester Stallone; keep up, Dad."

"Oh, very apt." Dad finally understood the joke and giggled to himself.

Still with a great big grin on his face, he said, "Come on guys, here are our keys; let us go inside. I am sure you cannot wait to see your new bedrooms."

It was a very tall, double door with a large, gleaming letterbox.

Matt whispered to Molly, "*The Shadow* will have no problem getting through this one!"

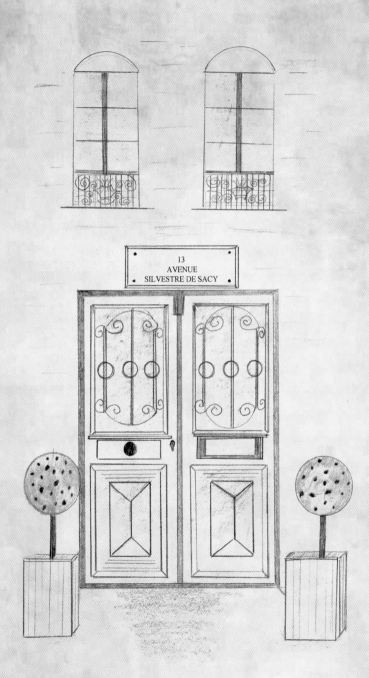

13
AVENUE
SILVESTRE DE SACY

Dad turned the key and, as they stepped into the hall, they were all amazed at how grand their new home looked, with an enormous, wide staircase fit for a king.

Mum could not believe what she was seeing - another hat and cane stand, just like in London and New York.

Matt said, "That will be handy."

Mum replied, "Yes, but only if you have a hat and cane!"

Dad switched on the electric and water and turned the heating on, as they could not take off their coats until the place had warmed up; it was very cold.

Mum and Molly went upstairs to look at the bedrooms, while Dad and Matt had a good look around downstairs.

Matt shouted, "Look! There is a huge garden with a conservatory; Mum's going to be pleased."

Mum and Molly came back downstairs extremely excited, telling the boys there were lots of bedrooms and three good-sized bathrooms, and the top floor had a roof garden.

Mum said, "The attic feels a bit spooky. I hope there are no resident ghosts."

Matt just looked at Molly and smiled.

Mum said, "I feel another book coming on."

Matt whispered to Molly, "So do I."

Matt and Molly carried their suitcases upstairs and decided which bedroom they were going to have. The house was fully furnished, with even bed linen. All Mum had to do was buy more towels for all their bathrooms.

Matt asked, "So where is all our furniture going?"

Molly replied, "To Nan and Grandad's house."

That evening they all went out for dinner. Dad ordered moules and frits for everyone, which went down well.

Matt said to Molly, "We have not seen our friend *The Shadow*. I wonder where he is?"

Molly replied, "Don't worry, I should think he is having a good look around."

Molly was right. On the way back, *The Shadow* was flying around the Eiffel Tower. People were looking up into the sky and pointing.

Mum said, "Look! It's an old black sheet that has blown off someone's washing line! At this rate, it will be fit for the bin." To their amazement, that is exactly where The Shadow landed, with a bent cane. Matt's and Molly's lips were sealed.

The next morning, Dad took them for breakfast and to do some shopping.

Matt went out of the door first to check on the bin, but The Shadow was nowhere to be seen.

Mum said, "I must clean the bin out when I get back; the previous owners left a lot of smelly things inside. At least in France they empty the bins every day. I heard them this morning about 6 am."

Molly whispered to Matt, "Oh no, that means he could be in the dustcart. I do hope he is all right."

As they were walking down the Avenue, people were smiling and saying, "Bonjour."

Dad replied, "Bonjour, parlez-vous anglais?"

Molly said, "What did you say to them, Dad?"

Dad replied, "I was saying 'good morning' back, and asking them if they spoke English."

When they arrived at the café Dad said, "You order breakfast while I go and get some cash."

Once they were seated at the table, all Molly could see on the menu was croissant and jam. When the waiter came over, she smiled and, remembering what Dad had told her, asked, "Parlez-vous anglais?"

The waiter replied with a French accent, "Yes, I do; what can I get you?"

Molly thanked him, and they all ordered eggs on toast with fresh orange and coffee.

"How did I do?" asked Molly.

Mum replied, "Very well. I think you both will learn the language in no time."

After breakfast, Dad settled the bill and then they all went to buy some new towels and other bits and pieces that they needed for their new home.

On the way back to the house, a dustcart drove past, and there on the back was *The Shadow*, going TAP, TAP, TAP with his cane.

Mum said, "Well I never, there is that old black sheet again; it looks as though it's moving."

Matt replied, "Without a shadow of doubt."

When they arrived home, they put all their bags in the hall, while Dad said he was going to make a cup of tea.

Molly said, "Cola for us please, Dad."

Dad went into the kitchen to put the kettle on and, as he turned, he thought he saw someone sitting in the rocking-chair, swinging back and forth. He rubbed his eyes and looked again. The person had gone, but the chair was still rocking slightly.

He mumbled to himself, "Perhaps not; I must be seeing things!"

He made the tea and drinks, then took them back into the lounge and put them on the coffee table.

Mum looked at him and asked, "Are you OK, dear? You look very pale, as though you have seen a ghost."

Dad replied, "You may well ask, but no, it was just my imagination."

Mum asked, "What do you mean?"

Dad said, "Well, I know this is going to sound stupid but, in the corner of the conservatory, I thought I saw someone; it looked very much like a monk."

Matt replied, "What? A chipmunk?"

"No, a monk that lives in a monastery."

"Did you see his face?" asked Molly.

"No, it was covered with his cloak and he had a shield of some sort in his hand," Dad replied.

Matt said, "Wow, here we go again!"

Molly said, "Well I sure hope we see him."

At that moment, there was a knock on the front door. When Dad opened it, nobody was there, but down on the floor was an envelope. Inside there were a card and a book. Dad said, "It says, 'Welcome my friends,' and is signed, 'Monsieur Claude'."

'Bonjour, bienvenue mes amis'

Monsieur Claude

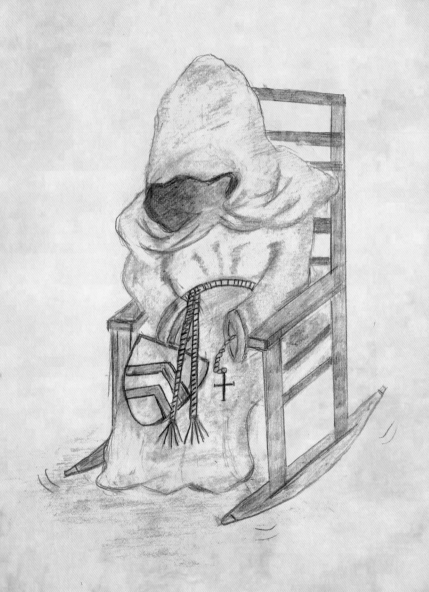

CHAPTER 2

BOOK OF HOURS

It had been a busy day, and the family sat down in the lounge in front of a roaring fire; which was just as well, as their heating system had packed up.

Mum said, "Pyjamas tonight, kids; it will be very cold."

Matt and Molly were looking at the book that Claude had left, but none of them knew who he was.

Dad said, "I don't start my new job at the bank for another week so, first thing tomorrow, I will phone the man about the heating and get it fixed; he has left his number on the boiler."

Mum said to the twins, "No school for a week, so you will be able to learn some new French phrases before you go to bed." They both said goodnight to their parents, and off they went to study their French.

"No dreaming of ghosts," shouted Mum.

"As if!" replied Matt.

Matt tried to read Claude's book, but was not having much luck as it was all in French.

There was a TAP, TAP, TAP at the window and, as Matt turned, there was The Shadow, standing on the balcony.

Matt went over to unlock the door, and said, "Hello, old mate, what have you been up to?"

The Shadow told him he had been flying around the Eiffel Tower and had met a new friend.

"Not again; who?" replied Matt.

"Well, look behind you; he is sitting over in the corner. He is an old monk," said Bertie.

"Not another chipmunk," replied Matt. He turned, gasped, then ran to get Molly. "Quick, hurry, come and see; you won't believe it."

They both ran back to Matt's bedroom and out onto the balcony.

"What's the big secret?" asked Molly.

The Shadow moved to one side and, sure enough, there in the corner sitting on the bench, was an old Benedictine monk.

"What's he doing here?" asked Molly.

"He is our new ghost, and what's the betting his name is Claude?" replied Matt.

Bertie's new friend stood up and said,

"Bonsoir, Matt and Molly; "

Molly stepped back and whispered to Matt, "What is going on? We seem to attract ghosts wherever we go. He must be the one that sent the welcoming note and the book."

"Yes," replied Matt.

Molly asked their new guest, "Parlez-vous anglais?"

"Yah, absolutely," the monk replied.

Molly said, "Oh my god, a posh monk."

Matt laughed and said, "At least he is not a chipmunk."

"I've heard it all before," chuckled Claude.

"Where do you live, Claude?" Matt asked.

"I live here Matt, on the top of the house, in the roof-garden shed. I love it there." His head was bowed, with his hood covering his face. On the side of his tunic was a shield.

Molly asked, "What's with the shield, Claude?"

He told them, "At one time, the monks here, just like in England, were knights of the realm, guarding the tombs of the Kings. Now, if you will excuse me, I am off to bed to rest; I have a busy day tomorrow at the Tower - money to be made."

Matt and Molly just stood there amazed and said, "How do you make money?"

Claude replied, "I stand on this little box, very still, and, now and again, I move or take a bow.

"The tourists are not sure whether I am a statue or real but, in my case, I am neither."

Claude told them that all the money he made he gave to the monastery for their funds, which kept the building safe and sound.

The Shadow said, "Yes, a mime; I remember seeing them in Covent Garden, in London."

Then up the drainpipe he went, two floors up to the roof garden, and disappeared.

Matt and Molly just stood speechless - they could not believe what they had just seen.

"Here we go again," said Molly.

They both went off to bed, but Matt sat up trying to translate the little book that Claude had left with the note. The Book of Hours was with the Gallery of Kings. But still Matt did not know what it was about.

Finally, he drifted off to sleep, with Bertie huddled in a chair in the corner.

The next morning Dad was up early, dealing with the heating engineer while Matt and Molly were still asleep.

Mum went upstairs, knocking on their doors and telling them to get up, as breakfast was ready. Molly was up as soon as she heard Mum, but Matt was dead to the world.

"Come on, wakey, wakey, rise and shine," pulling open his curtains at the same time.

After breakfast, the twins were going to go up and sit in the roof garden and study their French phrase-book.

Dad said "Au revoir" to the heating man, as the heating was now working, and Mum was busy in the kitchen baking cakes.

Dad said, "We still don't know who Claude is, but I am sure we will meet him soon."

"I'm almost certain we will, Dad," said Matt, and made a quick exit upstairs to join Molly in the roof garden.

The roof garden was amazing. It looked beautiful from the balcony, looking over Paris, and the Eiffel Tower felt as though you could reach out and touch it, as it was so close to Avenue Silvestre de Sacy. They were incredibly lucky to live in such a beautiful house.

7ᵉ Arrᵗ

AVENUE
SILVESTRE DE SACY

1758 – 1838

ORIENTALISTE

Matt went over to the old potting-shed; he opened the door, but no Claude.

Just then Molly shouted, "No! Look over there, at the bottom of the Tower. Just like he said, he is standing on his box, acting a mime and raising money for the monastery."

Matt said to Molly, "*The Shadow* should do that; he looks so good with his hat and cane."

"No, Matt, you must not say anything to him; you know how shy he is."

Matt just laughed. "Yes, you are right, Molly; I promise I won't say anything to him."

Mum came up with their lunch and said, "It is really beautiful up here, and a potting shed. I will be spending a lot of time in there. I see you have the little Book of Hours."

Matt replied, "I think it is interesting. It is full of prayers and psalms showing the labour of the months, together with the relevant sign of the zodiac."

"Yes, you are right, Matt; well done."

Dad was busy in the conservatory and, every now and again, the twins would catch him checking that nobody was rocking in the chair. This amused Matt and Molly.

Matt said, "I love that old rocking-chair."

Dad replied, "Yes; fit for a monk!"

That evening, they decided they would have a game of *Scrabble* after dinner and yes, once again, Dad was the winner.

Mum said, "Well, time for bed, guys, as tomorrow Dad and I are going to take you on an adventure to Musée de Cluny." They all said goodnight.

Matt got to the top of the stairs and said to Molly, "I think Dad definitely saw the monk, I mean Claude."

The twins decided to pop up to the roof garden and say goodnight to Bertie and Monsieur Claude. There he was, in the potting shed, counting the money that he had taken that day. The Shadow was lying on one of the shelves.

Matt said, "Hello; have you both had a good day?"

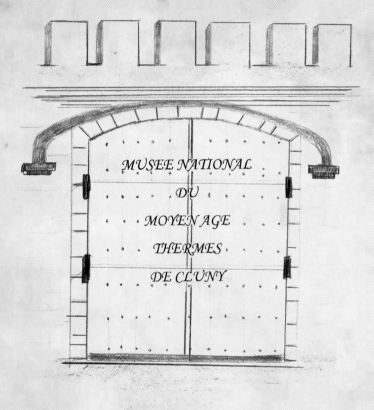

MUSEE NATIONAL

DU

MOYEN AGE

THERMES

DE CLUNY

"Yes," they both replied.

Molly said, "I wish we had some codes and clues to play."

Claude said, "Oh yes, Bertie has told me all about the codes and clues, and the old leather book. So tonight, I will set you some. I believe you are going to Musée de Cluny tomorrow?"

"Yes," replied Matt.

So, Claude and *The Shadow* set to work.

That night, Matt and Molly could hardly sleep they were so excited. How they enjoyed the codes and clues!

The next morning, *The Shadow* gave the twins a piece of paper and told them that Claude had to go to the monastery up on the hillside and hand over the funds he had collected from yesterday; *The Shadow* was going to meet him at the Tower.

Matt said, "Well, off we go again but, this time, we will have Mum and Dad in tow."

Matt and Molly looked at the piece of paper and, yes, these were good codes and clues.

MUSEE de CLUNY

A Baptist head you must find
An old man who is truly kind

The book of hours you must find
Only if you're timed

Don't lose your head
The King said

The bathroom is so cold
And many stories to be told

A fine lady hanging on the wall
With servants, so just call

A Tower of a different shape
And a King in a cape

BAPTIST/BOOKS/HEADS/BATHROOM/
LADY TOWER

The family were all ready, and walked out onto the Avenue. Dad noticed Claude standing by the Tower, and his mind flashed back to the monk sitting in the rocking-chair.

"No, it can't be," he sighed.

Mum said, "He is rather good; Molly, here is a euro go and pop it into his box."

Molly squeezed through the crowd and put the money into his box. The monk looked up, but no face to be seen, just a dark cloth. He nodded to say thank you. Everybody cheered and applauded.

Dad looked back at Claude, who just bowed his head.

Eventually they arrived at the Musée de Cluny, a medieval mansion with a plaque saying:

'Completed in 1500 by
Jacques d'Amboise'

Dad paid the entrance fee and they all walked into the grand mansion. Dad was given a map of the building and all the places of interest. Matt and Molly agreed to meet their parents back at the entrance in a couple of hours.

Matt went back and asked the lady for another map.

"Now, Molly, keep your eyes peeled. We have to find the BAPTIST. I think we should start in the courtyard."

So off they went. On the way, they read a sign on the floor, with an arrow saying 'To St. Johns'.

They saw three pillars, and the one in the middle had a plate which read: 'St. John the Baptist'.

"Yes," said Molly, "our first code. Let us carry on and find BOOKS." So, for this one, they decided to go back to the entrance with an arrow pointing up the stairs and saying 'Library'. When they reached the top, they could see so many shelves full of books everywhere.

Molly said, "We must find a special book, but which one?"

As they walked through the library, there in the middle was a glass cabinet, and inside were two incredibly old books named 'Hours', from the 15th century, and they had been there an exceptionally long time.

Molly said, "That's the one, our second code. Now, what does the third one say, Matt?"

Matt replied, "HEADS, and for this one I think we should go and have a look outside. It's funny we have not seen Mum and Dad."

Just at that same moment, they were walking past the café window and they saw Mum and Dad sitting down, having coffee. They spotted the twins and waved. Molly waved back and blew them a kiss.

"Typical! Always drinking coffee! Now let us see; where would there be any heads around here?" said Matt.

As they walked around the corner into another small courtyard, there was a plaque on the wall which read, 'To the gallery of Kings'.

Matt said, "That sounds interesting; perhaps one of the kings has lost his head!"

Over in the corner was a stone wall and, to their amazement, there were twenty-eight stone heads.

Matt said, "I thought we were only looking for one."

Then there, carved in stone, were the words:

'Kings of Judah 1220
during the reign of Philippe Auguste'

Molly said, "I think they're morbid!"

"So would ours be after all this time. We can definitely say we have found HEADS," replied Matt.

Matt asked Molly how many more codes to go, and which one was next.

She said, "Two more to go, and the next is BATHROOM. Now I do know that, in some places, the bathroom is known as the toilet, but I'm not sure about here in France."

Matt replied, "Well, toilet, bathroom, washroom, whatever, it will be a good place to start, so come, let's go inside."

The stone floors were so fine, with Roman words and dates. Then, on the floor, was the word 'Gallo', so they followed the signs and finally, in a doorway, was a sign: 'Gallo – Roman Baths'.

"Yes!" shouted Molly, "that is the BATHROOM. It says that the baths were built in AD200."

Matt replied, "Well I think the water must have gone cold by now."

"Very funny. The other door in the other room says 'Gallo-Roman Frigidarium', which are the cold baths," Molly replied.

Matt, being Matt, said, "I told you the water was cold."

Molly crossed the code off, leaving just one more, which was LADY TOWER.

They decided to go back upstairs, where the pictures and artifacts were. They loved all this so old and so bold; 'History' was the name of the place and, on the wall at one end, was a massive tapestry showing a unicorn sitting beside a beautiful lady.

Molly said, "That's it, our last code: LADY."

Matt replied, "She's old or, should I say, the tapestry is - 15th century. I have never seen a unicorn."

As they turned, Mum and Dad were walking towards them. Mum asked them, "How did you get on?"

"Excellent! All done; the codes and clues were well chosen," Molly said.

Mum asked Matt what he liked best of all.

Matt thought about this then replied, "The Book of Hours, but it was a shame they had no time to read it."

"Oh, very funny," said Dad.

As a treat, Mum and Dad decided to take them out to dinner, and afterwards, when they got back home, they still had time for their favourite game, *Scrabble*. As they were setting up the game, *The Shadow* and Claude joined them.

They all talked about their day and *The Shadow* announced that he was now the best mime at the Tower. Claude whispered to Molly, "He's good, but not that good yet."

They all said goodnight and Matt and Molly fell asleep dreaming about their Roman day out.

CHAPTER 3

KISS KISS

It was Sunday afternoon, and Matt and Molly were preparing for a French questionnaire that Mum was going to test them on. They knew many of the words, and had to use them in a sentence.

As they were working away, The Shadow tapped on Matt's window. Matt went over and let him in, asking, "Hi, Bertie, not working with Claude today?"

"He's got nothing to say, he is extremely quiet. Not like Cobweb Joe; I miss him so much."

Molly said, "Yes, we do, too, but he is in New York, a long way from Paris and, if you remember, it took you a while to get used to him."

The Shadow replied, "Why don't we write him a letter? I know he was going to be staying at the house during spring. Hopefully, he will receive it, and there is a chance he may come over. It is worth a try.

"Good idea," replied Matt. So, after their homework, they sat down and Bertie wrote the letter to their good friend, Joe:

Hi old mate
Hope you are feeling great

Has the house got new owners yet?
Lots of new furniture and a family pet

We all miss you so much
thought we would write and keep in touch

Paris is fine
Mum and Dad love the wine

A mate called Claude he is a monk
The shield he wears is not old junk

Standing still all day
You would not believe what people pay

A French mime from another time
A little shy but simply fine

Our Paris address is on the back
You're welcome to stay in our new shack

Love Molly, Matt, and Bertie

TAP, TAP, TAP…

They addressed the envelope and put a stamp on it, and *The Shadow* marched off to the post box.

That evening, Mum sat the twins down in front of the roaring log fire and marked their French test. The house was so quiet; Dad was busy in his study, preparing for his first day at the office.

"Well? How have we done?" asked Molly.

Mum replied, "Très bien."

"Did you hear that, Matt? We have done very well."

Matt and Molly said goodnight to their parents and went off to bed. They were thinking about the letter to Cobweb Joe. Molly thought that he would make an incredibly good mime.

Matt fell asleep thinking of all the good times they had spent with Joe, and that it would be great to see him again.

Monday morning arrived and it was a fresh, windy day. Mum told the twins that she would come with them on their first day and get them settled in. Their school was an old abbey.

Matt whispered to Molly, "I hope Claude is not teaching us."

Their day went so fast; their teacher was great and they had already started to make a couple of friends, but so much homework.

On Thursday evening they decided to go and say hello to Monsieur Claude, as they had not seen him or Bertie since they had started school.

As usual, Claude was counting his euros. He said, "I heard you are attending my old school. You will do very well at my old abbey. Bertie told me I should take a day off this week - seven days is too much."

Matt laughed and replied, "Yes, I agree; it is bad for your health!"

Claude said, "If you like, on Sunday we could go on another adventure and I will make up another set of codes and clues. What do you think?"

"Yes please," replied Matt and Molly.

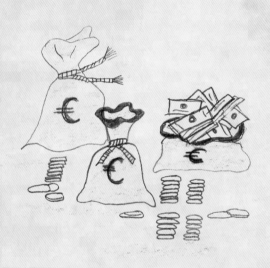

On Friday night, Molly had a fright when she heard a scratching noise outside her window. As she slowly opened the curtains, there was Claude, counting his money on the metal garden table.

Molly opened the door to the balcony and said to him, "Don't you ever sleep?"

He replied, "Why? We are ghosts - we don't need much sleep. By the way, I came here to give you and Matt the codes and clues for Sunday but saw your curtains closed, so I decided to sit here and count the takings."

Molly thanked Claude and said goodnight.

Sunday morning, Molly woke early and went to show the codes and clues to Matt.

After breakfast, Dad told the twins that he was taking Mum for a round of golf in the morning and, after, they were going to have lunch, if they both wanted to join them.

Matt said, "No, we are OK thanks, Dad. We have homework to complete and, anyway, it is too cold." It was a lovely, crisp, sunny day, simply perfect for codes and clues.

The taxi arrived to take the two golfers to the club and Matt shouted, "Hole in one!"

Dad replied, "Of course."

Once the cab was out of sight, the twins read the codes and clues.

KISS KISS

Kiss, kiss as the French would say
A map you must have for the day
Claude the monk said take the bus
It will be easier without the fuss
You must find a biscuit fit for a Queen
But never in Paris this will be seen
Off the bus at Musée d'Orsay
A chair fit for a king you might say
A raincoat you must find
On the chair it will be signed
Look at the place where Picasso sat
Where a violin will play
All your tears away

BISCUIT/RAINCOAT/PICASSO/VIOLIN/ KISS KISS

Monsieur Claude floated down the stairs and handed Matt and Molly a street map and 10 euros.

Matt said, "Do we need a map? **The Shadow** has never given us one."

"You will need one, trust me," Claude replied.

"Wait for me!" shouted Bertie.

They walked up to the top of the Avenue, and Claude told them they must start with a bus ride for the first part of the course.

Molly said, "It sounds like we are in a race."

They all jumped on the bus and Claude told Matt to ask for two single tickets to Musée d'Orsay.

Matt and Molly ran to the back of the coach, where they had a good view. **The Shadow** and Claude came and sat next to them.

Matt was looking at the codes, and the first one was BISCUIT.

Molly shrugged her shoulders and said, "No idea. It could be a chocolate one or a plain one."

As the bus drove down the side of the river Seine, they kept their eyes fixed on every sign, building and plaque until the bus came to a halt at the traffic-lights.

Claude said, "Well I never; what do you see over there?" Molly looked and saw a sign saying 'Assemblée Nationale Palais Bourbon'.

Matt shouted, "Yes, Molly! First code broken."

"Well done," congratulated Claude, with Bertie going TAP, TAP, TAP, showing his approval.

The bus drove off down the Quai Anatole and, after about five minutes, the driver announced over the speaker, "Musée d'Orsay."

Matt and Molly jumped off the bus and looked at the next clue, RAINCOAT.

Matt said, "Well, it is not raining, and there isn't a cloud in the sky."

Molly pointed and said, "Look, Matt, over there - Musée d'Orsay. I think we should go in and have a look."

Matt and Molly walked up to the entrance. It was six floors high and there was a sign saying,

'Built by Victor Laloux in 1900

For the mainline railway station

and from 1986 is now a Musée d'Orsay'

There was an entrance fee, but Claude told them to tell the man they were eight years old and that would get them in free.

Matt said, "Parlez-vous anglais?"

The man replied, "No, voilà qui est parfait."

Claude said, "He said that is fine and you can go in."

The man said, "Tout droit."

Matt said, "That means straight on."

"Well done," replied Claude.

Molly said, "Now let us find this raincoat." The museum was huge, and time was ticking away. They walked everywhere then, right at the end of the Grand Hallway they spotted a small room and, in the corner, was an old oak chair fit for a king. On the floor was a plaque, which read:

'Chair by Charles Rennie Mackintosh
from his tearoom 1900'

Matt said, "Mackintosh - that is the code. I can remember
Mum telling Grandad to get his mackintosh out of the
car. Another code broken, and only three more to go."

Matt and Molly went back outside, looking for the next
code - PICASSO. There was another coach ready to leave,
and the sign said, 'Musée Picasso'.

Perfect, they thought and, once again, sat at the back.

When everyone was seated the driver started the journey.
Matt said, "He did not take any money from tourists;
perhaps it is a courtesy coach."

"Brilliant! Not a euro spent," replied Molly.

They still had the 10 euros Claude had lent them.

Ten minutes later the driver shouted out, "Musée
Picasso!" Molly said, "That was an easy code; only two
more to go. The next one is VIOLIN. This should be
easy; we should hear the music."

Just inside the door of the museum was a plaque saying:

'Pablo Picasso 1881-1973
Built by Aubert de Fontenay in 1656'

"Molly, what is the next code?"

"I've just told you – VIOLIN; did you not listen?"

Once again, the twins got in for free, as there was a group of children on a school trip and so they just followed them.

Matt said, "That was a stroke of luck. Do you remember in London? We did the same there with the northerners on the boat on the Thames."

"Yes, no money spent," replied Molly.

The twins decided to look upstairs first and, in no time, they found a picture on the wall, of a violin and sheet music.

"Brilliant," said Matt.

The Shadow tapped his cane once again, and Claude tapped his fingers on his shield and said, "Well done, you two; now only one to go."

Matt and Molly walked down to the next floor, where there were so many amazing pictures. A large group of people was looking at one piece of art. The guide was talking in several languages, and the picture was called 'THE KISS, with Jacqueline Roque and Picasso in 1961.

"Well, that is the final one," said Molly.

Monsieur Claude clapped his hands and was so pleased that Matt and Molly had completed the codes and clues successfully.

"Now back on the coach and back home, hopefully before your Mum and Dad get back."

On the way home, Matt said to Claude, "I would love to go on a boat trip on the river."

Claude replied, "You must be insane." Matt and Molly both laughed.

Luckily, when they arrived home their parents were still not back. The phone rang - it was Mum, telling them that they were still in the golf club and that she had prepared their dinner and left it in the fridge with a note saying 'Homework', with a funny little face.

The Shadow and Claude helped the twins with their homework, and everything was completed just in time for their parents' return.

What a day they had had. It was time for bed, with a new week ahead.

"Bonsoir," was all that was said.

PICASSO

JACQUELINE

CHAPTER 4

LUXOR WILL TAKE YOU THERE

It was a cold February morning, and the twins were getting ready to start a new week. They had settled in nicely at the old Abbey and were starting to make new friends.

When they arrived home late that afternoon, they saw Monsieur Claude still at work raising funds for the monastery, but *The Shadow* was nowhere to be seen. Matt and Molly waved to their new friend and, as usual, he just bowed his head.

Mum announced that she had picked up a film for them all to watch, but first they had to tackle their homework and have dinner.

Dad arrived from his first day at the office, had a quick bath and joined the family for supper. He told them he had seen the monk again, standing on his box under the Eiffel Tower.

"I'm almost certain now that he was just like the one in the rocking-chair, no mistake. I must say the box was nearly full - everybody loves him."

Matt glanced at Molly and laughed.

"Why are you laughing, Matt?" asked Dad.

"Well, if you think he is the one that was sitting in the rocking-chair, perhaps you should charge him rent."

"Now that's a good point, son," replied Dad.

Mum said, "Right; let us watch this film - it is *The Hunchback of Notre Dame*."

Dad replied, "That rings a bell!" Not even a chuckle.

That week went so quickly for the twins and they were so excited, as Mum told them that their grandparents were coming for half-term. Mum told them that the French schools had more holidays than children in England, which pleased Matt and Molly. She said they would be arriving on Eurostar, and they would be picking them up from Gare du Nord station at 8.45 pm.

Matt and Molly were so excited when Friday night arrived, and Claude had prepared some codes and clues for another adventure.

Matt said to Bertie, "Do you know you are only three hours away from Old London Town?"

Bertie replied, "Yes, I know; perhaps this time I can return with your grandparents."

Once again Molly replied, "Most definitely not."

She remembered having a similar conversation when her grandparents visited them in New York. Matt and Molly would be lost if Bertie went back to London.

Matt and Molly studied the codes and clues, which read:

LUXOR WILL TAKE YOU HIGH

Across to New York Avenue you must go
Then find something rhyming with Tokyo

After a long walk
Find a place where people talk

Paris IV will make you come alive
Working from nine till five

Then a citrus fruit in a building you will find
Think smart and make up your mind

The next place will send you spinning round
But do not drop onto the ground

An aeroplane you must find but not in the air
So remember take good care

NEW YORK/PARIS IV/ORANGE/FUNFAIR/
AEROPLANE

Saturday morning arrived and it was still very cold. Everyone had a job to do, getting ready for their grandparents' visit.

Dad said, "Mum and I will go and pick some food up from the supermarket; what are you two going to do?"

They both decided they would like to go out on their skateboards. So, as usual, Mum told them to wrap up warm.

As Matt and Molly walked along the Avenue, they could see *The Shadow* and Monsieur Claude leaning up against a one-way sign.

Claude shouted, "Are you both ready, as today's clues and codes are going to be hard, without a shadow of doubt?"

Bertie replied, "Hey, that's my line!"

Matt said, "Yes, we are ready; let's begin."

Before leaving the house, Matt had picked up the map of Paris, and studied it while eating his breakfast.

Molly asked, "Where to first?"

"New York," replied Matt.

"What? We are in Paris," said his sister.

Matt said, "No, there is a New York Avenue; now follow me."

They jumped on their skateboards and off they went. Over the River Seine at Pont d'Iéna and, once they reached the other side, there in front of them was a sign saying 'New York Avenue'.

"Well done, Matt. The second clue is Paris IV."

Matt replied, "This is going to be fun; it's like the Yanks against the French. We will have to concentrate."

"Then go slower, or we might miss something," replied Molly. This pleased Claude, as he was a lot slower keeping up, whereas Bertie just floated along.

After a while, they noticed a building which was named 'Palais de Tokyo', but nothing to do with Paris IV, so they kept skating.

Matt and Molly were in awe of all the beautiful buildings.

Matt said, "Look - Avenue Churchill; now that sounds very English."

They decided to stop and rest for a while; next to them was the Grand Palais, but they were not allowed in with their skateboards. Monsieur Claude told them to go ahead, and he and Bertie would look after the boards. So, in they went, and not a euro spent.

They had a good look round and finally ended back at the magnificent entrance. The lady at the kiosk spoke very good English, and asked them if they were going without visiting the Université; "You may learn a lot about PARIS IV."

Matt glanced at Molly and said, "That's the code." They thanked the lady and had a look round.

Once they were back outside, there was no sign of Claude and Bertie.

Molly said, "Oh no, that can only mean one thing; this is going to be funny."

She looked at the codes and clues, and told Matt ORANGE was next on their list.

As they set off down the side street, there in front of them were Monsieur Claude and *The Shadow*, flying along on their skateboards. What a sight this was. They both looked at each other, and gave the boys a round of applause.

Molly said to Matt, "Now look out for something citrus, like oranges."

"OK," replied Matt.

Up in front was another musée, with people queuing to go in. Again, it said 'children go free'. Matt and Molly stood close to the couple in front, and the lady thought they were one family, as she handed them their ticket.

Matt said, "You will never guess, Molly; our tickets include a free drink and a cake. It must be our lucky day."

"Result! Paris is turning out to be one of my favourite cities," replied Molly.

They went up to the counter in the café; the waitress spoke fluent English and said, "Welcome to the orangery; what would you like to drink, and what cake?"

Matt replied, "Grande, s'il vous plaît, madame."

The waitress just laughed.

Molly had a big grin on her face, as Matt had not realised what the waitress had said - he was too busy getting his answer right.

"Did you hear, Matt? She said, 'Welcome to the ORANGERY.' That's our next code; well done us!"

After they had finished, Matt said, "I will get two Cokes to go, and I think we should get back to the boys on our skateboards before they have too much fun. Now the next clue says, 'the next place will spin you around'."

Molly said, "Could be a funfair."

As they walked towards the exit, the twins both said, "Merci beaucoup, madame. Au revoir."

Now Matt and Molly had to look out for a funfair and the boys.

As they walked down the side of the musée, *The Shadow* and Monsieur Claude suddenly came flying past on their skateboards.

Claude said, "Had lunch, I see." Molly was still eating the last of her cake.

She looked puzzled, and asked Claude, "Why do you have a shield, but no sword?"

Claude replied, "It is against the law. Swords are weapons of the past and must be kept in safe places, so we protect our history."

"That explains everything," she replied.

Claude said, "Now you have to find your funfair, so off you go."

"Can we have our skateboards back?" asked Matt.

Bertie and Claude turned and said, "On your bike," and, in a flash, they were gone.

"I told you, Molly, we will have to watch those two they are having too much fun."

As they walked along, they noticed a magnificent building up ahead. As they got closer, they saw a stone arch, just like the Arc de Triomphe near to where they lived. The plaque on the front said:

'Built by Napoleon 1806
and crowned with the horses looted
from St. Mark's Venice'

The twins were standing, admiring the Arc, when The Shadow went TAP, TAP, TAP with his cane, and asked, "What do you think of the Arc de Triomphe du Carrousel?"

Matt replied, "It is spectacular, but we are actually looking for a funfair."

Bertie said, "Yes, but it is only a clue; look closer at the plaque."

Matt shouted, "Of course, 'carrousel'! That is what they have at funfairs." Just then, Claude floated past and agreed he had made it a little harder, as they were getting rather good.

Matt looked at Molly and said, "Well, one to go. We have got to find an AEROPLANE, I presume?" Claude bowed his head, and The Shadow tapped his cane.

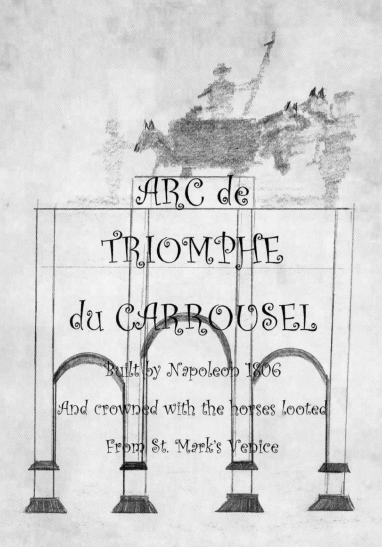

ARC de

TRIOMPHE

du CARROUSEL

Built by Napoleon 1806

And crowned with the horses looted

From St. Mark's Venice

Claude said, "Follow us, and your destination won't be far away."

They walked through the gardens of Jardin des Tuileries, where they saw many lovely flowers and trees, now with all the bees.

Matt said to Molly, "There are lots of planes above, but that can't be the clue." Just then, a bus drove past and stopped by the roadside. The driver announced over the loudspeaker that the tall, gold building was Luxor Obelisk, built by Louis XV in the mid-18th century.

Matt said to Molly, "But we are looking for an aeroplane, not a king's palace." Just as the bus started to move off, Matt noticed another sign; it read 'Place de la Concorde', which was where the Luxor Obelisk was situated.

Molly shouted with joy, "Yes! We have cracked it! AEROPLANE is Concorde, but not as we know it."

Claude pulled up on his skateboard and congratulated the twins on their code-breaking.

"Now back home for tea as, tomorrow, your grandparents are coming to stay."

Matt said, "I love Paris, but London is still my favourite."

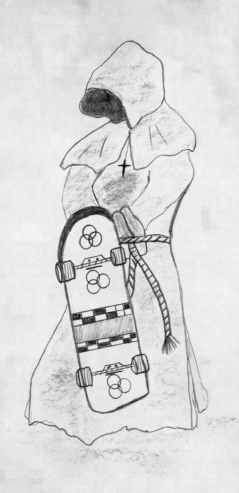

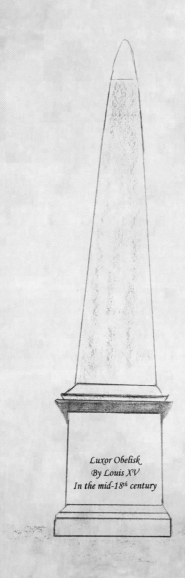

Luxor Obelisk
By Louis XV
In the mid-18th century

CHAPTER 5

A TASTE OF THE U.S.A.

It was Sunday morning, and the day had finally arrived when Nana and Grandad were coming to stay.

Mum was rushing around, cleaning and making up beds, so Matt and Molly were sent out for the morning until lunchtime.

They sat on the bench opposite the Eiffel Tower. Matt said, "Do you know?"

"Know what?" asked Molly.

Matt told her, "We have been here since New Year, and we have never been up the Tower."

"Yes, I know, but it is awfully expensive, Matt; it costs a lot, you know."

Meanwhile, Monsieur Claude was miming away, and the twins said good morning, but he had nothing to say.

At that moment, *The Shadow* just happened to be floating by and said to Matt and Molly, "He is upset, because now the bell on the monastery has stopped ringing and it will cost lots of money for the repairs."

Matt giggled and said, "Why doesn't he ask Quasimodo? I have a hunch he will be able to help. He lives in Notre Dame, just down the road."

Although Claude was sad about the repairs, he piped up and said, "Yes, he is good with bells, so I am told and, for cheering me up, I am going to treat you both to two tickets to go up the Tower.

Thank you, Matt and Molly."

The twins were delighted, and joined the queue after paying for their tickets. They decided to walk up the stairs to the 1st level. Afterwards, they watched a short film in the Cine Eiffel, all about the Tower's history.

Afterwards, they took the lift to the 2nd level; the views were breathtaking.

They decided to stay on this level, as up higher there was a thick mist, and they had such a good view from where they were.

Matt heard a man say, "You can see for forty-seven miles on a clear day."

Matt looked at the booklet that they had been given at the entrance, and told Molly that the Tower was built by Gustave Eiffel in 1889 and he was called 'the magician of iron'.

Then a lady told her daughter, "Look over there; that is where we are going tomorrow - Disneyland Paris."

Molly heard and said to Matt, "Now that is where I would like to go." As she turned, there in front of her stood *The Shadow*.

Bertie said, "Well, keep your fingers crossed; you never know."

Matt asked, "What do you mean?"

Bertie replied, "Your mum is always arranging things. I'm sure one day your wish will come true, and you know Claude and I will make up some codes and clues for any trip."

Matt said, "Brilliant, Bertie and, in the meantime, we can keep hoping."

They had such a lovely morning; a total surprise Claude treating them to tickets for the Tower, and now they had the excitement of their grandparents' visit.

As they left the tower, they could see Claude miming away, and he had such a large crowd. The tourists just loved him. So did Matt and Molly; they thought he was cool.

When they got back home, Mum was washing down the steps and Dad was busy cleaning the windows. "Well, spring has finally sprung; now, guys, let's have some lunch."

At 7.30 they all left to meet Nana and Grandad at the train terminal. Eurostar was due to arrive at 8.45. Matt and Molly were so excited. The taxi pulled up, and off they went to Gare du Nord railway station.

They decided to get a coffee in the little café opposite the platform while waiting for their grandparents. At exactly 8.45, the train arrived.

Nana and Grandad were two of the first to get off with their cases, and spotted Matt and Molly instantly; and, yes, Mum had a few tears while Dad ordered the taxi.

Matt and Molly's grandparents were so pleased they were now living in Paris - a lot closer than New York. They told the twins that they had arranged a special treat for them on Tuesday.

Dad suggested they all go out for dinner, and made a reservation at a lovely old French restaurant just down the road.

Nana said to Matt and Molly, "Our French is a little rusty, so you will both have to help us out."

As they reached the front door, Mum shouted, "Oh, no, no! Not again!"

Grandad asked her, "What's the matter, dear?"

Mum replied, "The old hatstand has the old hat and cane on it again."

Grandad said, "Well, it is either the kids messing around, or you really do have a ghost."

Matt coughed, and dared not look at Molly.

Mum was keeping her eye on the twins as they left for the restaurant.

That evening there was a lot of parlez-vous anglais, mainly by Grandad.

Mum told the twins that Nana and Grandad had a day trip planned, but it was a surprise, and Dad said he would book a day's holiday from work.

Molly scratched her head and said, "What is it, another muse? Or a day on the river? Or, perhaps, a French chateau?"

Mum said, "You will have to wait and see."

Monday was a day to relax, and Matt and Molly had been keeping diaries of their time in Paris. Molly had been sketching Claude and had got him off to a tee.

That evening, Matt was in his room when a note was slipped under the door. It was from Claude and Bertie.

They had been busy making up all the codes and clues for the outing on Tuesday. Matt went into Molly's room and they studied the note:

A TASTE OF THE U.S.A.

Downtown Main Street we must go
With lots of characters you might know

A French chateau fit for a queen
Or a mouse which should not be seen

Thunder mountain will take your breath away
When all the characters come out to play

It's definitely a wonderland some would say
But it is not in the U.S.A.

With flying elephants and a spinning cup
Come on kids, try your luck

While the Queen of Hearts is baking her tarts

You must take a journey through space
With puppets dressed in lace

So, a taste of the U.S.A. this will be
Just you both wait and see

STATION/SNORING/PARIS/MAD/SPACESHIP

Matt and Molly were up early on Tuesday morning, while all the others were still in bed. They made their breakfast and went and sat in the conservatory.

There was a strange noise coming from the old French cupboard. Matt went over and slowly opened the door.

"Bertie; what are you doing in there?" asked Matt.

The Shadow was hanging from an old coat-hanger; he did look funny.

Bertie said, "Monsieur Claude hung me up, saying it was a game, but he never came back. Normally I can do anything but, for once in my ghost life, I am truly stuck."

Just as Matt was going to help Bertie off the hook, Nana came in. Matt quickly shut the door, telling her he was just hanging up his coat as it was warm, as some would say. She quickly returned to Grandad in the kitchen, thank goodness.

Matt and Molly quickly went to rescue Bertie. Once unhooked he went flying out, hanger and all, out the door and straight up to the roof garden to Claude, for an explanation!

By this time, everybody was up and getting ready. Mum was giving orders, as usual, and getting looks from the family.

"Well, someone has to," she said.

Dad said, "Is everyone nearly ready? The taxi is now here."

Mum handed the driver a piece of paper, and it had their surprise written down of where they were going. She was determined to keep it a secret if possible.

It was a long journey outside Paris, and the twins could not believe their eyes. When they got closer, there in front was the big sign, 'Welcome to Disneyland Paris'. Now they were both excited.

Dad paid the driver. He told them to have a good day and said he would be waiting outside at 4.30 pm to pick them up.

Nana said, "I hope you both like our surprise. We thought of different gifts we could buy, but we thought this was the best."

"Absolutely," said two excited children.

Matt got out the codes and clues that he had been keeping in his wallet, waiting for the day they hoped they would go to Disneyland. They told the family that a close friend from school had given them the game to play.

"Great! We thoroughly enjoyed the last time we played the codes and clues in New York," said Grandad.

Molly said, "This is going to be brilliant. I can't wait to go on the big dipper."

Grandad got out his wallet and handed the tickets to the man at the kiosk, who gave them maps of all the attractions.

Just as they entered the park, there in front of them was Main Street Station.

"Brill, that is our first clue, Matt; good start," shouted Molly.

They walked onto the main platform, and there waiting was an old steam train.

"Quick, it is just about to leave," said Dad, and they all jumped in the nearest carriage.

Nana asked, "What is our next clue?"

Matt said, "Well, we have to have find someone or something sleeping, as the clue is SNORING."

The only person snoring, having a quick nap, was Grandad; Nan gave him a nudge. "Come on, sleepy-head, keep up."

The train chugged along, blowing out all the steam and, in the distance, was a fairy-tale chateau.

Mum said, "Cool! Chateau de la Belle au Bois Dormant."

Molly looked at the map and shouted to Matt, who had his head out of the window surrounded by steam. "Look! The second code - SNORING."

"What? Grandad?" Everyone just laughed.

"No, Sleeping Beauty, over there in the castle; that is her home."

Dad said, "I suggest we stop for a spot of lunch; escargot and frits."

Molly said, "No way. Snails, burger and chips for me, please."

After lunch, Mum told them there was another train ride waiting for them. So, once again, they all queued up. This time the train had no roof. They all jumped in the separate carriages, and off it went.

Molly said, "It sounds like thunder the way it is clattering along. Not knowing what she had said, the train slowly climbed up the mountain then, once it reached the top, the driver let off the brake, speeding back down the mountain.

Grandad's toupee nearly came off and Nana's false teeth fell out. Mum looked like she had been through a hedge backwards and Dad looked grey.

Well, Matt and Molly were laughing; they just saw the funny side. What an experience. Matt and Molly could have done the trip all over again, no problem. They loved it.

The train finally came to a halt back at the entrance. Thankfully, Nana found her teeth and Grandad straightened his hair. Matt was still laughing.

Grandad said, "You wait, my lad, till you grow old; you will have parts that will disappear." They all just laughed.

As they got off the train, the driver thanked everybody for visiting Thunder Mountain, and he said that he hoped they would see them again very soon.

Nana said, "Not on your nelly."

"What's a nelly?" asked Molly.

Nana replied, "Oh, it is just a saying, dear."

Matt whispered to Molly, "That's another code."

What? Nelly?" said Molly.

"No, silly, thunder; we heard it, but didn't see it,"

replied Matt.

"What is the next code?" Grandad asked.

Molly replied, "It says MAD."

Mum said, "Everybody at Disneyland is mad. The next place is Fantasy Land."

Nana said, "I hope there are no ghosts; I can't take them, in any shape or form."

Mum replied, "Don't worry, Mum; we have left them all back home." She just laughed; little did she know!

Matt said to Molly, "I have not seen Minnie or Mickey Mouse, or Pluto."

Molly replied, "No, and don't forget Captain Hook."

Then, as they were walking back down Main Street, the whole park came alive. All the characters came out to play. Everyone started clapping and whistling.

They had their pictures taken with Mickey Mouse in his house, and the twins dressed up, with more photos. Pluto looked funny with his big, black nose. Then Grandad had his photo taken with Captain Hook. The twins loved his ship, the gold-and-red galleon.

Mum said, "Well, I don't know about you lot; I would love to stop and have a cup of tea, but I think everyone round here will think I'm mad."

Dad said, "Look, over there; a perfect place for tea. It is The Mad Hatter's Tea Party." He was right - the attraction had big teacups to ride on, with a café opposite.

Matt said, "Well done, Dad, that is another code - MAD Hatter's Tea Party."

Molly said, "One more code to go; let us have something to drink and a rest, and we will have a think what it could be. SPACESHIP - that could be easier said than done."

So, for the next twenty minutes, everyone was trying to guess the last clue and code, while they drank their tea and Coke.

Mum said, "The last place on the map is Discovery Land, so let's go and discover."

They found a sign which read 'To Space Mountain, where you can go from earth to the moon.'

Grandad said, "Can't wait; we can put Nana on and see if she returns."

Molly said, "That is not very nice, saying that about your nearest and dearest."

Grandad told her he was only joking, and gave Molly a wink.

They all arrived at the entrance and a man said, "All aboard the spaceship for a ride to Star Wars."

They all held on tight, and what a ride that was!

Dad thought it was the best part of the day.

Matt and Molly could not choose; they just loved their day in Disneyland.

A perfect day was had by all and, just as the taxi guy said, he was outside at 4.30.

When they arrived home, Mum made some soup and homemade bread, which they all enjoyed while discussing their perfect day. They all agreed an early night was on the cards. Even Matt and Molly.

Just as Matt was nearly asleep, he heard a familiar sound of *The Shadow* going TAP, TAP, TAP, with his cane on the balcony. Matt went and opened the door, and there he stood, with Claude.

Claude asked, "Have you had a good day at Disneyland?"

"Yes, it was brilliant! You were right, Bertie, our grandparents did us proud; and thank you for the brilliant codes and clues - they made the day."

Bertie said, "Excellent! Now off to sleep, and sweet dreams all about the taste of the U.S.A.

TAP, TAP, TAP...

CHATEAU de la BELLE au

BOIS DORMANT

CHAPTER 6

BELLS WILL RING

Matt and Molly had a lovely time with their grandparents, but the week had gone too fast. Sunday night arrived, and they took them to Eurostar at the station and waved them goodbye.

The Shadow drifted over to Matt and Molly and said, "I wish I could have gone with them."

Matt replied, "So do we, Bertie."

As the taxi pulled up outside the house, Mum said, "Look! Up on the balcony; it looks like that monk that stands and mimes under the Tower."

Dad looked and said, "There is nobody there; now you are seeing things."

Matt nudged Molly, and not another word was said. But Dad had seen him, and he had, several times, but not said a word.

Mum reminded the twins that it was school tomorrow, so it was an early night.

Monday was a bright, sunny, spring morning in May. At school, the teacher asked them all about their holiday. Matt and Molly told the class about their grandparents' visit and their surprise trip to Disneyland Paris.

A few of the other children had been over to London, which was quite funny, as they had talked about all the places where Matt and Molly had been. They loved hearing about their home in England. They both wanted to tell them about *The Shadow* of Old London Town, then decided it was not such a good idea.

Every night after dinner, the twins carried on taking their homework up to the roof garden and sat with Bertie and Claude.

Claude said, "One day, I would like to travel to London and be a mime in Covent Garden, I dream of it so much, especially when tourists put money in my box and tell me that I would do well in Old London Town."

Matt said to *The Shadow*, "Watch out, Bertie; you have competition." Bertie just giggled.

Claude said, "I cannot be with you this weekend; I have to be at the monastery as the new bell is being delivered, but I have already completed the codes and clues, so you can take them with you when you go back down."

Matt and Molly said goodnight to their two friends and went back to their rooms, both thinking of the codes and clues; they could not wait for the weekend. If they looked at them too early, they would not be able to concentrate on their homework.

Mum was busy writing her new book, which was based in Paris, and about Kings and Queens and children's dreams.

Matt told Molly that he was still doing little sketches of their adventures, and Molly told him that she was noting everywhere they had been.

Friday finally arrived and so did the rain, so Mum told them that the order of the day was umbrellas at the ready.

As they walked along the Avenue, it was amazing seeing the Eiffel Tower towering above, and the rain was like a big shower falling over the iron framework.

Suddenly, it stopped and the sun came through, and a double rainbow glistened over the Tower.

All the tourists were busy taking photos, but no Claude, and not a shadow in sight.

Matt and Molly thought their day at school seemed to drag then, thankfully, 4 o'clock came and the old bell rang. Their teacher said goodbye to them in French and English, and told them to have a good weekend.

On the way home, Molly asked Matt whether they were going to do the next set of codes and clues on Saturday or Sunday.

Matt said, "It all depends on Mum and Dad; we will ask them when we get in."

That evening at dinner, Dad told Mum that he had to go into work on Saturday morning and help set up the new computer system.

Mum said, "No worries; I will carry on with my book. How about you two?" Molly told her they were sitting in the park and finishing their homework.

Matt said, "Brilliant! Now let's go and study the codes and clues."

BELLS WILL RING

To Pont St. Michel you must go
Then to the Island Ile de la Cite
Built 2,000 years ago

A medieval building you must find
And point zero a mark of some kind

A glass rose of red and blues
And gargoyles will give you the clues

You must find pieta and it is not bread
So please do not be misled

You must listen out for the bell
With a name you might know well

Houses with manuscripts that read well
With treasures which will never sell
REMEMBER THE BELL

ST.MICHEL/ISLAND/ZERO/ROSE/
ALTAR/BELL

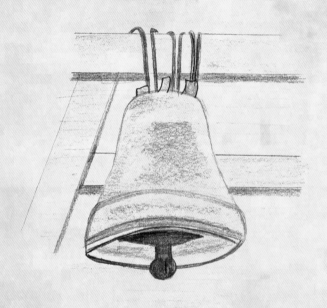

So, on Saturday morning Matt and Molly had breakfast, Dad wished them all a good day and Mum went to write more of her book.

Matt and Molly quickly put on their coats and Matt picked up Dad's map. As they were going out of the door Mum shouted, "You have forgotten your homework," and passed Matt their notebooks.

Matt said, "That was lucky; thanks Mum, how silly of us."

They shut the front door and Molly said, "Now we have to carry them around with us."

Just at that moment, Claude was sliding down the drainpipe.

"Good morning you two, so you are ready with your codes and clues. I can't come with you, as it is a busy day for me."

Matt replied, "Yes, looking forward to them."

Claude asked, "What are the books for?"

Matt replied, "Well, one is a map of Paris, and the other two are our homework."

Molly said, "Claude, please would you do us a favour and look after them for us?"

Claude replied, "Yes, of course; I will put them into the pocket behind my shield and you can collect them later." He said goodbye and went off down the Avenue towards the Tower.

Matt looked at the map and then the clues. It said they had to go to Pont St. Michel, and the map was directing them to go towards the East.

As they walked along, *The Shadow* came floating by.

"Hi guys, are you on your next adventure and, if you are, may I tag along for a while?"

Matt replied, "Of course, Bertie; we must find Pont St. Michel, then the Island Ile de la Cite.

It is 2,000 years old."

The Shadow said, "Well, I have found the first code; look over there - a sign 'Pont St. Michel'."

Molly clapped her hands. "Well done, Bertie!"

Then he just disappeared out of sight.

They walked past a man playing a guitar, and Matt dropped a euro in his hat.

"Merci," the man replied.

Molly said, "We must find this Island, but where would we find one around here, in Paris?"

Matt checked the map again and said, "Further down the Avenue is the Island in the middle of the River Seine."

Just up ahead of them was a road-sweeper; he kept trying to pick up an old Coke can, but it kept blowing around. Matt did no more; he stamped on the Coke can, picked it up and handed it to the road-sweeper.

The man spoke good English and thanked Matt, and asked them if they were there on holiday.

Molly said, "No; we live here in Paris; it is a day out for us. Please can you tell us where Île de la Cité is?"

The man laughed. "Yes, you are standing on it."

Matt replied, "But it doesn't seem like an island."

The man said, "There is water all around, with a roadway. Have a good day, and do not forget your shadow."

"Pardon?" replied Molly.

He told them the sun was casting a shadow behind them, giggled to himself and went on his way.

Matt said to Molly, "Brilliant! Now we have the second code – ISLAND. Come on, let's find the third clue. Oh, and bring your shadow with you!"

"Very funny," Molly replied.

Further ahead they saw a cathedral; it was enormous.

Molly said, "Now that does look very old, and it looks medieval."

"Yes, you are right; now we must find Point Zero," replied Matt.

As they got nearer the building, they could see a queue of people waiting to go inside. As the people moved along, just to the left of them they could see a large granite stone, with words carved out, it read:

Notre-Dame

A gothic masterpiece

Where Pope Alexander III

Laid the first stone in 1163

Marking the start of the

170-year build

Matt said, "That is a long time. Just imagine, the men who started it would not have seen it finished. That's quite sad."

As they got closer to the entrance, in the middle of the square, on the ground, was a star made from stone; it read 'point zero' and all distances were measured from this.

Molly said, "That is another code; we are doing well. The next clue is ROSE."

Matt and Molly continued to look all around them, on the ground, up in the air. They looked at the main doors and two towers.

Molly said, "Look! There are the gargoyles, up on the gallery; now, where is the rose?"

The large glass window above was beautiful, and a little boy standing next to them had a pair of binoculars.

He said to his mum, "Look! The window is all reds and blues; this must be the West Rose Window, and there is another one - the South Rose Window."

Molly nudged Matt and whispered, "That's the code; now the next one says ALTAR."

Matt and Molly reached the entrance and were once again ushered in with the people in front, who paid for a family ticket and it was thought the twins were with them. So, they both got in free again, which was a stroke of luck.

They walked round until they came to the Treasury.

Matt said, "Loads of money."

This time he was wrong, as it was not paper money, but precious objects. Now they were on the lookout for the next code.

Matt said, "Perhaps we should look out for a wedding party."

Suddenly, they found themselves at the high altar and the carving of Pieta's statue by Nicolas Coustou.

"Yes, here is your pitta bread, as you call it. They are two more codes. Only two to go."

They decided to have a look at the booklet they were given when they came into Notre Dame, and tried to find where the bell would be. It said the bell would ring in the south tower, but not by Quasimodo, the hunchbacked bell-ringer of Notre Dame.

It was a minute until midday, and people were gathering outside in front of the cathedral, so Matt and Molly joined them and, sure enough, the bell rang.

What a morning they had had, with all the treasures they had seen - they would remember them for evermore.

As the bell rang for the last time, they saw Bertie hanging from the upper gallery with the gargoyles, going TAP, TAP, TAP, with his cane.

Everybody clapped, and he just bowed his head.

Matt laughed and said, "He is definitely spending too much time with Monsieur Claude."

Molly replied, "I agree."

They both arrived back just in time for a late lunch, and Mum asked where their homework was.

"Oh no, we have left it at the tower gardens," replied Molly, and dashed out of the door.

She saw Claude doing his magic, and had to wait in the queue.

She whispered to him, "Homework, please."

Claude replied, "Euro, please." Molly dropped a coin into his box and thanked him once again for looking after their homework.

When she arrived back home, Mum said, "That was lucky; someone could have taken your books."

Matt winked at Molly, and quickly asked what was for lunch.

Mum replied, "Croque Madame, otherwise known as cheese and ham toastie with an egg on top."

Matt replied, "Yum, yum."

Molly whispered to Matt, "This afternoon we have got to get down to some serious homework, and some noting and illustrations for our new book."

At that moment, Bertie came floating through the kitchen and said, "Well done on another set of codes and clues. I have been dreaming about Old London Town."

Matt said, "One day, Bertie, we will all be back there." Bertie said nothing, just floated upstairs, and all they heard was the sound of his cane.

TAP, TAP, TAP...

CHAPTER 7

ON YOUR BIKE, BOYS

Matt and Molly had been working extremely hard and, with only one more week before the school holidays, they were getting ready for their exams.

They spent the next three nights up on the roof garden with Claude and *The Shadow*, who was thinking he could not wait to be back in London.

Claude would test them every evening in preparation for their exams.

After their stressful week, it was time to say goodbye to their classmates. All Matt and Molly could think about was being able to stay in bed, lots of television, and exciting adventures with more codes and clues. What was there not to like?

Dad announced that they were going to take the twins for a week away, a special treat for working so hard. He had to finish a couple of reports at work and then they could enjoy their surprise.

Claude and Bertie heard what he said and decided it would be a good excuse for another set of codes and clues before they went away.

"Yes please," said the twins.

Friday night arrived, and The Shadow was lying on Matt's sofa in his room, moaning about Claude.

"He wants me to be a mime every day over the holidays, as he has got a target for raising the funds for the monastery, but I get so bored!"

Molly said, "Come on, Bertie, this is so unlike you. It will get you out and about, and you will be raising money for a good cause."

Bertie replied, "You are absolutely right, Molly, sorry for being such a pain. I am missing London so much, it's all I can think about. I must step up and see it as a kind thing to do."

"That's the spirit," replied Molly.

Bertie said, "I will go and tell him yes, and ask him if he has completed the codes and clues." Off he went, going TAP, TAP, TAP.

On Saturday evening, Claude left Matt and Molly a note:

Dear Matt and Molly,

I am going away on holiday and would appreciate if you could keep an eye on Bertie. Please remind him to put the money in the gate box at the monastery.

Goodbye my friends, now turn the page and see the codes and clues for your next adventure,

A bientôt, Monsieur Claude

That evening after tea, Matt and Molly went upstairs to study the new set of codes and clues that Claude had left them. They were going to miss him. They had got so used to having him around. Just like Cobweb Joe. They wondered how he was, and what tricks he was getting up to.

Now, down to business - they picked up the note and it read:

ON YOUR BIKE, BOYS

It could be boys or girls you might say
Bikes are the order of the day
A building which is in the U.S.A.

Next on the list is Pont de l'Alma
So, do not go fast
With a flame that will always last

With a Princess memorial
Who we loved and so adorable

Now on our bikes we must go
To see a very local show

The next stage of the race
You will join in and embrace

The winner will be a lot thinner
And a jersey will go to the winner.

U.S.A/OLD FLAME/CHAMPS/YELLOW

Matt said to Molly, "Well, it looks like we have to get our bikes out."

Sunday morning arrived and Matt pumped up the tyres on their bikes, and told their parents they were off on an exercise and they would see them later.

The twins stood outside the house and read the codes and clues once again, but could not work out the first clue and where to start. They looked up, and there in front of them was *The Shadow*, on his way to the Tower.

Matt read the clue to Bertie, and Molly asked him what his thoughts were.

He replied, "I think I know, but I cannot tell you as it will spoil your adventure. All I will say is follow the Seine to Pont de Grenelle. Look up high above and your code will be broken."

They both thanked Bertie and wished him good luck with his miming at the Tower. Off they rode on their bikes, through the Eiffel Tower gardens then down to the Quai de Grenelle.

Eventually they arrived at their destination - It was the Statue de la Liberté.

U.S.A.

Matt said, "It is the same as the one in New York City."
On the plaque it read:

'Built by Gustave Eiffel'.

Molly said, "It is the same man who built the other one; he was a very busy man."

Matt said, "Brilliant! That is the first code broken - U.S.A. Now what is next, Molly?"

Molly replied, "FLAME is the second code, so we must now go to Pont de l'Alma."

Matt opened the map and told Molly that they had to go back the way they came. So off they rode, past the Eiffel Tower, and back home to where they started.

Molly said, "We have got to find an old flame, but we must not blow it out. Then a Princess memorial. So, what is that all about?"

They looked all around, hoping that something would jump out at them, but nothing. They decided to ride across the bridge over the River Seine and on the other side of the road, where they saw lots of tourists taking photos.

The twins pushed their bikes over to where the crowd stood. They noticed a plaque, which read:

'To the French Resistance fighters
For their Bravery'

The statue was an old flame, never to go out.

One lady said to her husband, "It is also a memorial to Princess Diana, who died in the car crash with Dodi Fayed in the Paris tunnel."

Matt piped up and said, "Yes, old flame!"

"Don't be horrible, Matt; Princess Diana was lovely."

"Yes, I know; only me acting the fool."

They were well pleased with themselves.

Matt said the next clue was a local show, but 'champs'? Nothing sprang to mind. So off they went on their bikes, until they came to a coffee shop, outside which were a lot of bikes, so they stopped to see what was going on.

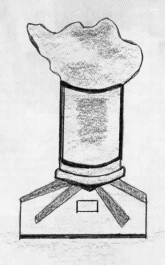

THE

LIBERTY

FLAME

Next to them stood a little old lady, and she turned to the twins and asked them if they were going to take part in the race, as this year was going to be the Champ of champs.

"No, but thank you for helping us with our clue."

All the crowd were talking about the race; then the twins realised it was the Tour de France.

"One more clue - YELLOW," said Molly.

As they were riding along by the river Seine, the pathways started to fill up with tourists and, at the side of the road, were railings with signs on and adverts.

They stopped for a rest, and there was a young English family.

Matt said to them, "Hi, guys, are you on holiday?"

They smiled at Matt and Molly, and their mum said, "Yes, we have come to watch the race; it will be interesting to see who wins the yellow jersey."

Matt replied, "Have a lovely day and enjoy the rest of your holiday."

Matt was so pleased, he said, "Well, Molly, I do believe it's the end of the Tour de France!"

The twins had a lovely afternoon; they had such a good view. The bikes came flying past at some speed. What a show! Everyone was clapping and whistling as they rode through, ending across the finish line at Champs-Élysées.

Matt said to Molly, "Come on, Sis; race you home."

"What's the prize?" asked Molly

Matt replied, "Burgers and fries, and the loser buys."

"You're on," laughed Molly.

Finally, they arrived home and Matt was the winner. They put their bikes in the shed and, as soon as they walked through the door, Mum said,

"Just in time; I will treat you both to lunch - burger and fries."

Molly said, "Oh, yes please."

Matt whispered to his sister, "You owe me one!"

What a fun morning they both had.

They decided to go up to the roof garden and tell Bertie all about their adventure with the codes and clues, and check how he had done with his first day miming for Claude.

As Matt and Molly walked through the door, they stood speechless. There was Bertie, sitting counting his euros and wearing a yellow jersey. He said to Matt and Molly, "Look guys, I won a yellow jersey. You are looking at the winner of the Tour de France – without a shadow of doubt."

TAP, TAP, TAP...

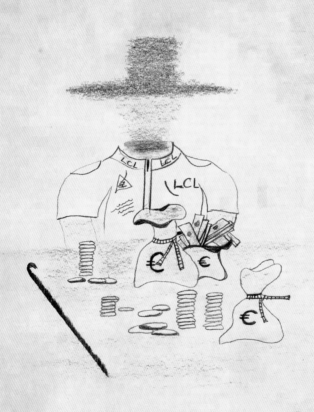

CHAPTER 8

NAPOLEON'S RETURN

Matt and Molly were enjoying their breakfast when Dad announced, "I will finish my reports on Friday, so next week we can pack and off we go."

Matt and Molly were even more excited.

Matt said, "I need a bit of a rest, I don't know about a holiday."

After breakfast, they went upstairs and were out on Matt's balcony when they spotted Monsieur Claude walking down the Avenue.

Matt shouted, "Hello, old mate, how are you?"

Claude replied, "I am worn out; the monastery needed a lot of sorting out. They know I am a ghost, but they also know I earn the most. The bells are back ringing nicely and the roof is fixed, so now it is only the heating to do."

Just then, *The Shadow* floated down and said to Matt and Molly, "I thought you were going on holiday this week."

Molly replied, "No, Bertie, a change of plan; it is next week."

Claude shouted up, "Excellent, as I have already completed another set of codes and clues for your next adventure."

He took the piece of paper out from behind his shield pocket, and a gust of wind blew it up into the air.

Suddenly, Bertie quickly jumped up, caught the codes and clues and handed them to Matt and Molly.

"Well done, Bertie; now I must be off to the Tower, as I am running a little late," shouted Claude.

Bertie was well-pleased that he could be of help, and he said goodbye to the twins and floated off up to the roof garden.

Matt and Molly sat down and studied their next codes and clues.

NAPOLEON'S RETURN

Wigs are the order of the day
Hiding bald heads some might say

De Cotte will blow you away
In gardens where you might play

You may go North, South, East and West
So, think of this place as a kind of test

A gold dome will let you in
Most definitely plenty of bling

Now six coffins on top of each other
But only one person, oh brother!

WIGS/BALLS/COMPASS/DOME/RETURN

Matt said to Molly, "I didn't even know Napoleon was lost!"

Molly replied, "Me neither, but I am certainly looking forward to finding out why."

After tea that evening, they went up to the roof garden to see the boys.

Claude said to *The Shadow*, "Well done, Bertie, you did a brilliant job while I was away; you made loads of euros for the monastery's heating system. Thank you."

Bertie was so pleased Claude appreciated what he had done, and was slowly warming to him. Molly was right - it took him time to get used to Cobweb Jo, and Claude was no different.

Molly said, "They won't need a heating system yet; it is summer, so you will have plenty of time to raise the money."

Matt said, "Well, we will say goodnight to you both. Well done, Bertie, once again, and we shall let you know how we get on with our next adventure."

The next morning the twins got up early, but Mum had already been up for two hours, writing in her study.

Matt opened her door, and told her they were going out to watch the boats on the River Seine and would be back around lunchtime.

She was busy typing away. "OK, have a good morning, and see you both later."

Matt and Molly walked down the Avenue, past the Eiffel Tower, and sat on a stone wall overlooking the Seine.

Matt said, "The clue is 'WIGS for old bald men'; that should be easy, but which way should we go?"

The twins sat for ages, just watching the boats going up and down the river. They were both looking back at the Tower when they noticed a film crew, filming lots of people dressed in clothes from the 18th century, and horses & carriages.

Matt said, "Did you see that? Let's go and have a closer look."

Matt and Molly were standing quite close to the film director, and heard him talking to his camera crew.

"Now I have already said you cannot take a shot of the Eiffel Tower, as it was only built one hundred years ago."

The director looked around and said, "Look over there, Avenue Silvestre de Sacy, that is perfect."

Without thinking, Molly said, "That's where we live."

Just then, six men walked out from a caravan, all wearing wigs, and were told to walk down the Avenue then get into the carriages.

Matt said, "That's it, Molly, WIGS! We have broken the first code."

The film crew continued filming as *The Shadow* floated down the Avenue, and just as Claude was walking down the steps of No 13.

Suddenly the producer shouted, "Cut! Cut!" Then, to Matt's and Molly's amazement said, "No, carry on. Look at those two - the old monk, he looks good, and *The Shadow* fellow is going to be a star."

Matt and Molly could not believe what they were seeing, and Bertie and Claude were enjoying the attention until they had had enough of the director shouting out "Cut!" every five minutes. They decided to float off, leaving the producer and camera crew stunned.

Matt and Molly had such a good time watching the film crew outside their house but, if they were going to be back home for lunchtime, they had to get on.

So, at the end of the Avenue, they stopped to look at the next clue. It said, 'de Cotte will blow you away'. And the code was 𝓑𝓐𝓛𝓛𝓢.

Matt looked at Molly and told her, "I don't want to be blown away." So they both looked at the map, and it showed gardens designed by Robert de Cotte, so off they went.

Eventually, they arrived at Rue de Université and they were mingling with lots of students who had gathered for their test results.

Molly said, "We should be getting our results soon."

Matt replied, "Hopefully all As."

They finally left the students behind and kept walking when, up ahead, they saw Musée de l'Armée. They had a good look round, but no 𝓑𝓐𝓛𝓛𝓢 to be found. Not even Frenchmen playing on the ground.

After walking a while, they came to the Invalides Gardens. There they saw bronze cannons from the 17th and 18th centuries. They were amazing. At the end of each cannon was a large bucket of cannonballs.

"Yes, that's the one! Second code in the bag."

Molly said, "Now we have to use our sense of direction; it says COMPASS, but which way should we go - north, south, east, or west?"

Matt replied, "I don't know, but this place Invalides seems a very interesting place, and it has lots of buildings; so, let us go and see."

Molly said, "My gut feeling is telling me to go south."

The twins walked through the beautiful gardens and there, in front of them, was Musée de l'Ordre de la Libération, it looked just like a mini-chateau.

Once again, there was a queue of people. Once inside, they were given a little notebook explaining all the items on show in the museum.

Matt and Molly walked from room to room and there, in a long corridor, was a glass cabinet.

There were many items belonging to General de Gaulle, and medals honouring the men and women who had been heroic during the Second World War. Right in the middle was General de Gaulle's liberation order and compass.

Matt whispered to Molly, "Code three broken; now let's go outside, I think a can of Coke and a bag of crisps are on the cards. I think we have earned them."

The sun was so hot, the twins sat under an umbrella in the shade. Just opposite, on another table, was another English family, telling their children about the church over at the end of the gardens. They told them that the church had a gold dome and crypts, and took twenty-seven years to build.

Molly said, "Excellent! Another code, and we did not have to move an inch."

Once the twins had finished their refreshments, they walked up to the church to look at the dome. There in front of them was a crowd and, to their amazement, Monsieur Claude was doing his thing.

Everybody loved him and was dropping euros into his box.

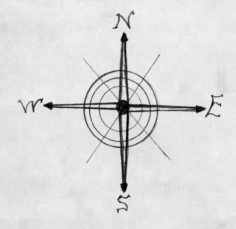

Matt and Molly walked forward and whispered to their friend Claude, and asked, "What are you doing here?"

Claude replied, "This is another pitch of mine. Now, how are you doing with your codes and clues?"

Matt said, "Good. We are on the last one now - RETURN."

Claude said, "This one is a hard one; six coffins you must find, but not all in a line."

"Matt said, "OK, we are ready for a challenge. See you later, Claude."

Claude said to Molly, "Aren't you forgetting something?"

Molly laughed, and dropped a euro into Claude's box. He just bowed his head.

Molly said, "I should know by now; I get caught every time."

Matt and Molly went inside the domed church and were behind crowds of tourists. There were so many crypts, with kings and queens who had been the powerhouse of France and beyond.

There was a tour guide with a microphone, telling everyone about the history. They finally arrived at the most important crypt of all.

The guide said, "This is the crypt of Napoleon, whose wishes were to have his ashes scattered on the banks of the Seine. He was originally buried at St Helena, but later was exhumed and brought back to the domed church where, today, you can see the Emperor Napoleon's body in his final resting-place. It is called:

'NAPOLEON'S RETURN.'

Matt said, "Look, Molly! On the plaque it also says that Napoleon's body was encased in six coffins and finally placed in the crypt in 1861."

Claude was proud of Matt and Molly completing their task, and asked them to help carry his box back home. When they arrived back, Mum and Dad were having a nap.

Molly said, "Can't wait to get old, Matt!"

NAPOLEON'S RETURN

Napoleon's final resting place

His body was encased in six coffins

and placed in the crypt in

1861

CHAPTER 9

LOUVRE DOORS WILL LET YOU IN

The following week went so fast, and Mum started packing the cases for the holiday break.

Molly asked, "Where are we going? Is it far?"

Mum replied, "No, not far, but I'm not telling you; it will spoil your surprise."

Monday morning came round so quickly, and Bertie was in a right state; he had lost his cane. He was pacing up and down in Matt's room when the door opened, and Matt's Dad came in. Bertie quickly hid behind the curtains.

Dad said, "I nearly broke my leg; I have just fallen over the cane on the stairs. You and Molly should not leave it there, Matt, it is dangerous."

"Sorry, Dad," replied Matt.

The curtain moved and Dad went over and pushed it back, and Bertie moved with it. Dad looked out of the window and noticed Monsieur Claude walking up the Avenue.

He said, "Everywhere I go, I see old monks."

Matt replied, "Well, Dad, there is an old monastery up on the hill just outside Paris, and they come down regularly for their supplies."

Dad said, "Yes, you are right. Anyway, the taxi will be here in an hour, so you and Molly must be ready." Dad went downstairs, still looking puzzled about seeing Monsieur Claude.

Matt tapped the cane and Bertie came out from behind the curtain.

Matt said, "That was close; please look after your cane."

The Shadow told Matt to have a good holiday and said they could look forward to more codes and clues on their return.

Molly walked into his room. "Are you ready, Matt? Mum said we had to pack swimming costumes, so I think we must be going to the seaside."

Matt replied, "I don't think so; not if it is just an hour away. Perhaps it is the Seine?"

The taxi arrived on time, and they all got in while the driver put their luggage in the boot.

The driver said, "Center Parcs, here we come."

Matt said, "Dad, what is Center Parcs? Is it camping?"

Dad replied, "Just wait and see; you are both going to love it."

The journey took longer than an hour because of the holiday traffic; it was so busy.

Eventually, they arrived in a forest.

Mum said, "It is an incredibly special place."

Matt replied, "I'm sure it is camping!"

Then in front of them was the gated entrance. It was as if they had stepped into a wonderland. They were given keys to their cabin, and the driver drove them to right outside their door and said he would see them Friday afternoon. The twins were speechless.

The place was so busy, with families all having fun on their holidays.

Matt and Molly went bike-riding. They loved the rock-climbing, and the birds of prey were brilliant.

The glass-roofed swimming pool was so much fun, with the rapids and water-shoots. The food was to die for. They could not have wished for anything better. Mum and Dad had done them proud.

Their parents had a good rest, Mum was pampered daily, and Dad played many rounds of golf.

The five days went so quickly and, as promised, the taxi driver arrived on their day of departure to take them back home.

On the way back, Mum asked them, "Well, how was that for a holiday?"

"Brilliant! We would love to go back again; thank you, guys," they both replied.

Due to the heavy traffic, it was late when they eventually arrived back at the house, so an early night was in order, and they both fell asleep dreaming of their amazing holiday treat.

On Saturday morning, everyone lay in, but were woken by the binmen.

Dad said to Mum, "Oh, no; I am late for work!"

Mum said, "Not until Monday, you're not. You have another couple of days off."

Dad was relieved. "Love it," he said.

Mum decided she would pop to the boulangerie and pick up fresh bread and croissants.

As she walked past Matt's and Molly's doors, she knocked and said, "Come on, sleepyheads, breakfast is on its way."

Molly jumped up and dressed, and there, on the floor, was a note from Monsieur Claude and *The Shadow*. They had left the twins the next set of codes and clues, so she put them in her bedside drawer, ready for her and Matt to read after breakfast.

Mum returned from the bakery and, as she hung her coat on the hatstand, a gust of wind blew the hat and cane off the hook and they disappeared through the letterbox.

Well, she rubbed her eyes and thought to herself that she was seeing things. She stood perfectly still, but all she heard was TAP, TAP, TAP. She opened the front door, but there was nothing to see. Still questioning what had just happened, she went and prepared breakfast.

Dad walked in and sat down, glanced over at his wife, and asked, "Are you OK, dear? You look as though you have seen a ghost; you look so pale."

"Yes, I am fine," she replied, and never mentioned a word.

Matt and Molly ate their breakfast, and Molly told Matt that Claude and Bertie had left them another set of codes and clues. After breakfast they went into the conservatory and played a game of *Scrabble*.

There was a knock at the front door. Mum went to open it, hoping there was not a hat and cane on the floor. In fact, it was the postman; he said, "This letter has been returned to sender, as it has an English stamp on it."

Mum thanked him and, noticing it was Molly's handwriting, gave her the envelope.

Molly made some excuse and said, "Oh, how silly of me! It was my old school friend in New York - we agreed to keep in touch."

Mum handed her the letter and told her she had a stamp in her bag. She asked Molly, "Who is Cobweb Joe?"

Molly replied, "Oh, just a nickname for my friend." She addressed another envelope and put the correct stamp on, and then told Matt she was off to the post office to catch the next post.

"Are you coming?" she asked.

"Yes," replied Matt.

On the way back, they bumped into *The Shadow*.

The twins were so pleased to see Bertie; they had missed him, and Matt told him all about the letter.

They told him that they had sent it off again and, this time, with the correct stamp. They all hoped Joe would get it, as they were missing him and wanted to hear how he was doing.

When the twins got back home, they went and sat in the conservatory and studied the next codes and clues, which read:

LOUVRE DOORS WILL LET YOU IN

The Louvre doors will let you in
With a glass roof and you will spin

A Renaissance portrait you must find
Which Leonardo da Vinci signed

Horseshoes you may find so be on your guard
In the glass-covered roof but no ordinary yard

This picture is from Holland in 1665
With clothes so fine bringing them alive

Find the man called Mr Pots
With all the monks there will be lots

A bird made of sugar and extremely sweet
But stone cold without a tweet

GREENHOUSE/SMILE/GIDDY-UP/
NEEDLES/POTS/SUGAR

Mum and Dad seemed to be busy, so Matt and Molly told them they were going for a walk down by the river, and they would see them later.

Mum shouted out, "Back for tea at 6.00, please guys."

Matt said, "Come on; it is 1.30 now, so we'd better get moving."

The Shadow said he would come on their adventure and help them, as Claude was busy at the Tower.

Yes, there was a monk at the Tower, but it was not Claude. Bertie said it was his twin, on holiday from Italy.

Matt said, "Well, we cannot wait to meet him, but now we must concentrate on the codes and clues."

Molly said, "I think the first one will be easy we have to go through some Louvre doors, and they are not far away."

So, off the three of them went and, in no time at all, the clues led them to the Louvre. Again, there was a long queue, with people waiting to get in.

The Shadow said, "Follow me." Matt and Molly stayed close to Bertie, who was going *TAP, TAP, TAP* with his cane, and they were at the front in no time.

The man at the kiosk looked at Matt and Molly, asking them where their parents were.

Suddenly, Bertie tapped his cane and spun round, pushing Matt and Molly through the entrance. Before the man could speak, he rubbed his eyes and, for that split second, could not make out what was happening, and carried on with the next family.

The Shadow said, "Not a euro spent."

Matt said, "Hey, that's my line!" Bertie just laughed.

Molly said, "First code is GREENHOUSE."

Matt said, "What? That rather large, pyramid-shaped building all made of glass?"

Molly replied, "Yes, that must be it. Well done; now, Matt: SMILE."

"Why?" asked Matt.

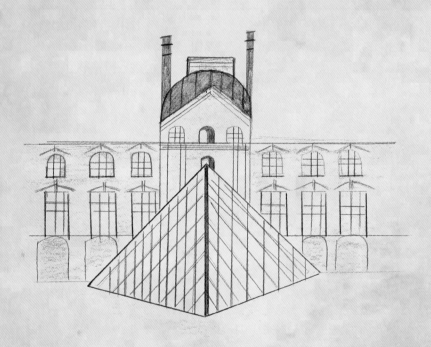

"No, silly; not you, the code. It is a portrait by Leonardo da Vinci, and it is signed," Molly said, "We have got to look at every painting and, don't forget, smile."

They walked from room to room but, in all the pictures they saw, the people looked miserable, with not a smile in sight.

There was a coffee shop, and Matt said to Molly,

"I'm just going to the loo; can you get us all Cokes and some cake?"

Molly replied, "Money, please."

Matt said, "I have none."

Bertie said, "Here are ten euros. I always keep them in my pocket for a rainy day."

"Well, that is a result, considering it is a lovely, hot, summer's day!" joked Matt.

Bertie replied, "You know me and my old sayings."

"Yes, and we love you for it, Bertie; thank you," replied Molly.

As they were eating their cake and drinking their Cokes, they saw one of their friends from school. They were talking about a lady smiling, called the Mona Lisa.

"I wonder if that is it?" asked Molly.

Bertie said, "Well, we won't know unless we go and look. Come on, you two."

Then Molly shouted, "Found it!" and there it was - the Mona Lisa, signed by Leonardo da Vinci.

Bertie said, "Right. Code number three is GIDDY-UP."

Molly said, "Perhaps we should look for horses."

Matt said, "This Leonardo da Vinci was a busy person; all these paintings, from Italy to France, and buildings."

The Shadow said, "The clue says a glass-covered courtyard. Look! There is one over there."

Molly said, "Now we must look for horseshoes, and we must be on our guard; and don't forget 'giddy-up'."

All the people who were walking in the opposite direction were commenting on the Marly Horse!

Then, directly in front of them, was a man and his horse and, on the plaque, someone had written the words GIDDY-UP.

Matt shouted, "Brilliant! Another code and clue broken."

Bertie checked the codes and clues, and told them they had to find NEEDLES.

He said, "This picture is from Holland, with clothes so fine."

They decided to go upstairs, and there were pictures hanging everywhere. As they walked along the hallway, they came across a painting of a lady making clothes. The picture had a brass plaque saying:

'Lacemaker 1665 Jan Vermeer
A glimpse of everyday life of needlework
From Holland'

Molly said, "Brilliant! Now we only have two more codes, and the next one says POTS, which could mean anything. However, it does say lots of monks."

Matt laughed and said, "Perhaps we will see Monsieur Claude and his gang!"

They decided to listen carefully to what all the other people were saying as, sometimes, other tourists would give them the answer. And, yes, they were right to do this, as a little girl said to her parents, "I did not like the monks with the shields. I thought they looked eerie."

Molly said, "Great! We are close. I wonder if it is Claude and his mates?"

As they all walked into the old chapel-like room, there were eight monks, carrying a knight in armour.

Molly said, "Yes! We have done it; but where is POTS?" Then she looked closer at one of the plaques; it read:

'This is the tomb of Philippe Pots from
The 12th century'

"Well done us."

Bertie said, "One more to go; it says:

A Birdman made of sugar so sweet
But stone cold without a tweet

Molly said, "I don't know if he's someone I want to meet, but I don't mind the sweet!"

Matt said, "Let's find the bird; this should be easy, because it says stone, so it won't be flying around from room to room."

Just as Matt had said, there in front of them stood an eagle on a stone pedestal. It was all carved in gold, and was called 'the eagle of sugar'.

Abbot of St. Denis
Made it back in the 12th Century

Bertie said, "Well done, you two; you have done well. But no sweets, so the bird had the last laugh."

Matt said, "Very funny."

Mum and Dad asked, "Had a good day?"

"A LOUVRE DAY!"

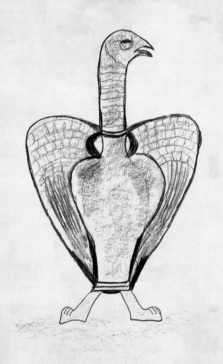

THE LOUVRE'S COLLECTION

OPENED TO THE PUBLIC IN 1793

Mona Lisa

By Leonardo da Vinci

Marly Horses

By Guillaume Coustou

The Lacemaker

From Holland 1665

Tomb of Philippe Pot

By Antoine le Moiturier

Suger Abbot of

St. Denis made

For King Charles V in 1380

CHAPTER 10

UP, UP, UP AND AWAY

The school holidays went so quickly, and the new school year had started.

Matt and Molly had been given their exam results, and both decided they would wait until they got home to open them.

The day seemed to drag but, eventually, they arrived home and, as they walked through the door, Mum shouted, "Well? How did you both do in your exams?"

Matt said, "Let's find out, shall we?"

So, they sat down at the table. Molly gave a sigh of relief and said, "Yes, I have got As and Bs. Then Matt opened his, and he had got the same. The twins were nearly bursting.

"Well done, you two; you deserve those results, as you have worked so incredibly hard. Dad will be pleased.

"Dad and I have a special surprise for you both at the weekend, for doing so well."

The week went so slowly and, even though September was here, it was still busy with visitors around the Eiffel Tower, which pleased Claude and Bertie.

Matt said, "I would like to try miming. I think it would be a cool job to have during the holiday."

Molly asked, "What would you be?"

"A knight in shining armour, with a sword," replied Matt.

Matt and Molly went up to the roof garden to do their homework and to see how the boys were.

Monsieur Claude was extremely happy, as he had reached his target and more for the new heating system at the monastery, with a helping hand from *The Shadow*. He was so grateful that Bertie had agreed to help him. Now the monks would have a very warm winter.

As they walked through the door Claude said, "I hope you have both got good results?"

Claude and Bertie knew the answer without asking really, as they knew how hard the twins had worked every evening after school. Their faces gave it away, as they were beaming like the cat that had got the cream. Another one of Bertie's sayings.

Molly said, "Guess what? We have a surprise at the weekend for doing so well."

Claude replied, "Yes, Bertie and I know what it is; you will be blown away!"

Matt said, "Come on, Claude, spill the beans!"

Claude said, "No, that will spoil your surprise. All we can say is that it will be well worth the wait."

Bertie said, "Claude and I have made up a good set of codes and clues for all of you - more like a test.

Molly said, "What; even Mum and Dad?"

"Of course! It will be fun, just you wait and see," replied Claude.

Friday night arrived, and Matt and Molly had a fright. They found Bertie in a right old state; he had managed to wrap himself around the chandelier hanging on the landing, and could not free himself.

The twins knew they had to get the stepladders out of the shed, and before Mum and Dad started asking questions.

Matt asked Molly to hold the ladders steady while he climbed up to the same level as Bertie. He managed to unhook his cape and unravel him from the light until he was free. As he came down, he flew off into Matt's room.

Just at that moment, Mum came through the hall, looked up at the stairs and said, "What on earth are you two doing?"

Matt quickly answered, "Cleaning the bulbs, as the dust was casting a shadow and stopping the light."

To Matt and Molly's surprise, Mum said, "Well, while you are doing that, perhaps you can do the one in the lounge as well."

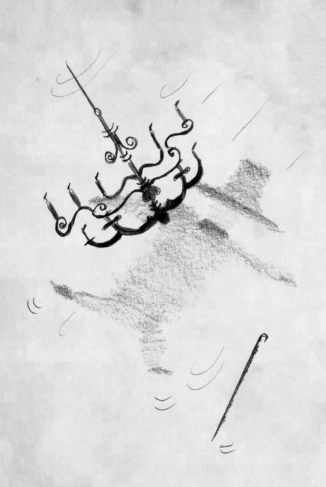

Matt did not argue. He thought about it, and thought this was a perfect moment to score some brownie points. As he walked past his room, he glanced at Bertie and said, "Now look what you have got us into."

Molly smiled at Bertie and said, "He's only joking."

That evening, Claude knocked on Matt's balcony door and asked, "Matt, I wonder if you could help me, please? I have these very heavy bags of money; I wonder if you would mind taking them up to the roof garden for me, otherwise I will be up and down the drainpipe all evening."

"No worries, Claude; give them here."

Claude thanked Matt and told him that he would leave the next set of codes and clues ready for their early start in the morning.

When Matt had returned from the roof garden, he grabbed the codes and clues, and off he went to find Molly.

The twins took their codes and clues, or test paper, as Claude called them, into the conservatory and studied the questions before they showed Mum and Dad.

UP, UP, UP AND AWAY
WATCHING THE EIFFEL TOWER SWAY

QUESTIONS

1. The Arc de Triomphe will come into play, commissioned by the man who won Waterloo.

2. The Hotel de Ville is not what is seems;
   with no beds, what is there instead?

3. The name of the windmill below. Even the sails stay still when it blows.

4. Who was Louis Pasteur?

5. This children's character is made from metal and you must say the name twice.

6. The artist with only one ear.

7. What was the old currency before the euro?

8. What do gargoyles do on a medieval cathedral?

9. Who was married to Pablo Picasso?

10 New York City towers over Paris.

11. What is held on 14th July?

12. Paris is made up of what?

13. Now back to the Tower, designed by whom?

The family were up extra early on Saturday morning and, after breakfast, Mum said, "Well; are we ready to go to the park?"

Molly whispered to Matt, "We're going on the swings."

"No way," answered Matt.

They walked down the Avenue, past the Eiffel Tower and they could see, in the distance, six hot-air balloons. Mum pointed at them and said, "Look, guys; one of them has our name on it."

Matt and Molly could not believe what they were hearing; one of their dreams was to ride in a hot-air balloon.

"Wow! And to think you thought it was the swings, Molly," said Matt teasingly.

As they got closer, Dad looked unsure and just kept saying, "Oh, it will be just fine."

They walked over to the first one, where a man was taking tickets. Mum had bought theirs online and gave him the details. The man stamped their tickets and told them they would be leaving in five minutes.

They were all helped in, one by one, and, when safely inside, Matt handed out the questionnaire and told Mum and Dad it was just a bit of fun and was like the codes and clues. He told them to look through them as, when they returned home, they would see who had scored the most.

Mum said, "Brilliant! But how did you know we were going in a hot-air balloon?"

"We didn't; that is what's so weird. I must have dreamt it."

Mum and Dad were both quite anxious about going up in the balloon, and they did not really question about the papers that Matt and Molly had brought along, thank goodness. After all, how would you tell your parents it was Claude and Bertie, the two ghosts that had been living in their roof garden? They would never believe them - or would they?

Matt and Molly held on to the sides of the basket. The balloon was amazing, in blues and golds. It was enormous when you saw it up close.

It slowly ascended, way up high, then floated directly over the Eiffel Tower.

Dad said, "What an amazing view; how good is this?"

Mum replied, "I will let you know when my feet are back firmly on the ground."

Matt said to Dad, "I love our surprise, but I don't know whether Mum is so sure."

Molly said, "Right! Out with our questions. Let us see how many we know."

Dad took his out of his pocket, and the wind took it straight out of his hand. So, Matt and Molly decided to share.

Matt looked down; he could see Claude and waved. Claude looked up and bowed his head, and he saw Bertie hold up his hand and tap his cane.

The first question was all about the Arc de Triomphe, which now they could see clearly, with all twelve Avenues going into it.

Mum seemed a little more relaxed now, and was getting use to the balloon. Mum and Dad really enjoyed the questions; it made them focus and made the trip much more enjoyable.

The next question that was on their list was 'New York City towers over Paris'.

Mum was not sure, whereas Matt and Molly new the answers, from their recent adventures. The next minute, Mum looked down and, just at that moment, she noticed the Statue of Liberty. She quickly wrote down the answer and said nothing.

They were floating across Paris for over an hour and finally started to descend, arriving safely back at the Tower Gardens. There were many people queuing for their rides and, as they touched down, everyone applauded and the cameras were going crazy.

That evening after tea, Mum said, "Right; get your questions and answers out." The family had answered all questions correctly, and Matt and Molly thanked their parents for such a lovely surprise. What a perfect day!

Claude and Bertie had their best day ever. So, everyone at No 13 Avenue Silvestre de Sacy was happy and looking forward to autumn, which was just around the corner.

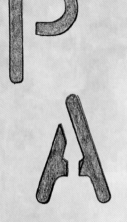

UP, UP, UP AND AWAY

ANSWERS

1. Napoleon in 1806

2. Town Hall or City Hall

3. Moulin Rouge

4. French chemist and microbiologist

5. Tintin

6. Vincent van Gogh

7. French franc

8. Stops water from eroding mortar in masonry walls

9. Jacqueline Roque

10. Statue of Liberty

11. Bastille day

12. Quarters

13. Gustave Eiffel

174

CHAPTER 11

THE SHADOW
A GHOST OF THE PAST

Autumn had arrived, and all the leaves were changing colour and starting to fall. All the French gardeners were busy pollarding the trees, which meant giving them a short haircut.

At breakfast, Dad told Matt and Molly that he was going to London for a couple of days as he had business meetings, and he was going to stay with their Nana and Grandad.

Mum said, "I wish we were coming with you, but Matt and Molly have school and I have to finish my book before Christmas. I cannot believe I have just mentioned that word; it is only eleven weeks away."

As the family were having this conversation, floating down the stairs was Bertie; he heard what was being said and decided that he was not going to miss this opportunity, so he quickly opened Dad's suitcase and hid inside. "Eurostar here we come.

Just at that moment the taxi had arrived outside, and everyone was hurrying Dad along and saying their goodbyes.

That evening after school, Matt and Molly went up to the roof garden to finish their homework. They asked Claude where Bertie was, as they had not seen him.

Claude replied, "He did not come to the Tower today, but I did not think anything of it as it was very windy, and I thought he would give it a miss today."

Matt looked for *The Shadow* everywhere, and then Mum asked what he was looking for.

"Oh, just my homework," he replied.

Mum said, "By the way, Matt, I have a letter here for you; it is from New York. It must be Molly's friend, Cobweb Joe."

Matt thanked his mum, and ran upstairs to show the letter to Molly.

They sat on the end of the bed and could not open it quickly enough; they were so pleased he had written back.

Hi Guys,

Good to hear from you, I miss you. The house is still empty, which is a stroke of luck as it keeps my bones warm.

I hope my old mate Bertie is keeping well and I hear you have another ghost, called Claude. They must be driving you both mad.

Going to a Halloween party next week, so that should be a hoot. Will get myself some new hats! Hope you like the picture!

Make sure you write again soon

Love ya dudes, keep cool

Cobweb Joe xxx

Matt said, "That's brill! I am glad he wrote back. I do miss him; it would be great if we could see him again."

Molly said, "He sends his love. Do you think he is coming over?"

Matt said, "Not sure. Now, where is *The Shadow*?" The twins could not find Bertie anywhere, so off to bed they went, dreaming of Cobweb Joe and his letter. One thing was for sure - Bertie would be pleased that he had written back.

The following morning there was still no sign of *The Shadow*, so the twins went off to school, looking forward to the evening when Dad was back.

Matt and Molly walked past Monsieur Claude, who asked about Bertie.

Matt said, "No, we cannot find him anywhere. We are a bit worried now."

The day at school went so slowly. Molly just sat at her desk looking out of the window, watching an old man playing French boules with his friends. And Matt was trying to work out where Bertie could be.

The bell rang, and the teacher told everybody to remember their homework, as it had to be handed in tomorrow.

On the way home, the twins were looking for Bertie, but no luck. When they got back, Claude had already finished at the Tower.

The twins could not concentrate on their homework, as it was so unlike Bertie just to disappear and not say a word.

Mum came through into the conservatory and told the twins that Dad would be home first thing in the morning.

Matt could see through to the hallway, and was upset that he could not see the hat and cane hanging on the stand.

The next day, when the twins returned home from school, Dad was there to greet them at the front door.

He said, "Nana and Grandad send their love, and London is still the same. I must say I do miss it, although it is good to be back in Paris with you guys."

Matt and Molly both said, "We miss it, too."

Later that evening, Matt and Molly sat at the top of the stairs and they could hear Dad telling Mum about his trip. He said, "I went round to the old house in Nightingale Square while I was there. They are putting up these new glass buildings everywhere.

"Our place was all boarded up, and your Mum was right - they are planning to knock it down. I know the company who is negotiating, so I went and made some enquiries."

Mum said, "I think it is Grade I listed."

"I know and, if that is the case, they will not be allowed to knock it down."

Matt heard what he said, and looked at Molly and said, "They cannot knock it down, it is where *The Shadow* and his wife live; it is their home."

There was still no sign of Bertie, and Molly said, "He must have gone on holiday."

"No, he would have said," Matt replied.

This upset the twins; they could not bear to think about it, and took themselves off to bed.

Mum and Dad were still discussing the house in London.

"I would love us to buy it; the only problem is all the glass buildings they are building round it."

Mum replied, "I don't mind. I think we have to try, even if it does need a lot of work. I think it would be a lovely project, and the twins would love it."

They both decided it was worth pursuing, so they would keep digging until they got some answers, hopefully the ones that they wanted to hear.

Meanwhile, back in London, *The Shadow* and his wife were having the same conversation, discussing Nightingale Square. She told Bertie that she had found some old plans up in the attic. The plans showed that it was once an old jailhouse, before the Victorian house was built.

"It says that there is a doorway on the south side which leads to the dungeons, and there is a tunnel which goes all the way down to the river Thames."

Bertie said, "This is such good news! It will have to be listed, as it is history, so there must be something in the garden to show this."

So out they went to have a look. Bertie floated round the garden, but there was nothing. He then went down the side of the house, where the bins were kept, and noticed an old wooden trapdoor. It was just like pubs have, where they keep the barrels.

The only reason this was showing was that someone had stolen the paving which would have been covering it up.

Bertie said, "Now what do we do?"

Bertie's wife said, "You must take this back to Paris and show Matt and Molly. They will then show their parents, who will do what is best."

Bertie replied, "You are right, my dear. I will stay one more night and return to Paris in the morning."

With that, they turned and floated up the staircase.

The next morning, Bertie was up early. He rolled up the maps and plans, and hid them in his cane. He said goodbye to his wife, and waved until he was out of sight and all she could hear was her Bertie's cane going TAP, TAP, TAP. Oh, how she missed him.

He arrived at Waterloo station; the place was buzzing, but he was going nowhere as the French were on strike for a day.

He had to spend a night at Waterloo, and floated up to the roof and joined the pigeons, who were quite amused by his presence.

In the morning, he woke early to the sound of a train pulling away out of the station. He grabbed his cane and managed to jump on the back of the train, thinking to himself, "Paris, here I come."

Three hours later, he was back in Avenue Silvestre de Sacy and looking forward to seeing Matt and Molly.

Just as he floated up the steps, he saw Claude coming home from the Tower. They were both pleased to see one another, and Bertie told him all his news.

Claude said, "One day, London is calling, and Covent Garden would suit me just fine."

That evening, when Matt and Molly were doing their homework, there was a tap on the balcony window.

Matt opened the curtains and shouted to Molly.

"Quick, Bertie's back! Thank goodness! We were getting really worried - where have you been?"

Bertie replied, "I have been up to London to visit the Queen."

Molly replied, "Very funny."

The Shadow told them about his trip, and told them everything he had found out about their old house in Nightingale Square.

Matt said, "Where are the maps now?"

Bertie replied, "I left them with Claude, up in the roof garden."

"What are we waiting for?" said Molly.

So, off the three of them went to join Monsieur Claude on the roof garden but, when they got up there, Claude had left a note saying he had been called to the monastery and would be back in a couple of days.

Molly said, "Oh no! We need the map, but we will have to wait until he comes back."

Matt said, "I don't know; we lose one shadow of the past, then you're back, and now we lose another.

"By the way, Bertie, we received a letter from New York, from Cobweb Joe, while you were away, and he sends his love."

Bertie replied, "There will be more ghosts than humans in the house soon."

Molly asked, "Yes, but how would he get here?"

Matt replied, "UPS, of course; it's the only way, and ghosts don't pay."

The end of the school week had come round so quickly, and they were still one ghost down.

In the evening, Matt and Molly were doing their homework when they heard a banging noise out on the balcony.

He shouted to Molly, "Claude is back, and he's having trouble going up the drainpipe."

They both rushed upstairs to the roof garden, just as Claude climbed over the railings.

Matt said, "Oh, are we glad you are back!"

Just at that moment, *The Shadow* appeared. "Hello, old mate; how are you doing? I was telling Matt and Molly about the maps. Do you have them?"

Claude said, "Of course! Sorry, Bertie, I forgot I had them - they're in my shield pocket."

The Shadow showed them to Matt and Molly, and they all sat round the table discussing the best plan of action. They all agreed that the adults had to be involved, so they would wait until weekend and then have a chat with Mum and Dad.

Molly said, "We thought you were going to be a shadow of the past; we are so pleased to have you back, aren't we guys?"

"Without a shadow of doubt," Matt replied, and Claude picked up Bertie's cane and went *TAP, TAP, TAP.*

13

NIGHTINGALE
SQUARE

CHAPTER 12

A WINTER WONDERLAND

That evening, after long discussions the twins, Claude and Bertie agreed that Matt and Molly would try and broach the subject with their parents at the weekend; that was not going to be easy to explain.

The Shadow rolled up the old maps of London and placed them, hidden, in the top of his cane.

Outside, there was no mistaking autumn had arrived. The leaves had all fallen from the trees, the branches were bare and the north wind did blow.

Bertie had decided to stay indoors, as it was extremely cold for him. He put his hat and cane up on the stand, and floated up to the roof garden to see his old chum, Claude.

For the next couple of days, Mum and Dad were constantly talking about Nightingale Square, and Dad was waiting on replies to all their questions.

Matt and Molly were back at school, and it had been a tough year, learning French and another culture, moving, and making new friends. But, despite everything, they had done well. They were so lucky they had Claude, who helped them with their French.

It was Friday, and the end of another week. Matt and Molly were walking home when it started to snow. It was now the beginning of December, and they only had two more weeks left before the Christmas holidays.

That evening, Claude told them that he had completed another set of codes and clues. He said, "It is not far to go and, with all the snow, I have changed the name to 'Winter Wonderland'."

The Shadow asked Matt and Molly whether they had heard any more about their house in London.

Molly said, "No, and we are not sure how we are going to tell Mum and Dad."

The Shadow said, "Just wait and see; leave it to me." And, with that, Claude gave them their codes and clues and told them to enjoy their adventure, so off they both went.

A WINTER WONDERLAND

To Versailles you must go
To gardens in white snow

A dragon you must find
But do not worry, he will be kind

You can see yourselves in this pool
But do not be like the king, a fool

A small chateau will sit opposite the canal
Where you must take a bow

Exotic plants all around
But no oranges to be found

DRAGON/POOL/CHATEAU/ORANGES

Saturday arrived and, after breakfast, the twins told their parents they were going out to have some fun in the snow.

Dad said, "In the old shed up on the roof, I remember there was an old sledge hanging up."

Matt said, "Brill! We can really have some fun now; thanks Dad."

They went up to the roof garden and, sure enough, there was the old sledge. Claude helped them get it down, and told them to keep safe and have a lovely day.

Molly said to Claude, "You must be cold up here. Why don't you come into the house and stay in our airing cupboard? It's huge, and you will be nice and warm in there."

Claude thanked them, and was so happy he had found somewhere warmer than the shed.

Matt and Molly pulled the sledge through the snow and went to the beautiful gardens in Versailles.

Mum decided that, while the kids were out, she would do some cleaning ready for the Christmas decorations to go up.

As she was hoovering the hallway, the cable got caught around the hat stand and knocked the stand over.

The old cane rolled across the floor and hit the front door. She put the hat back on the stand and went to pick up the cane but, to her amazement, the silver top came off in her hand. She could see something inside, so she tapped the end and the maps fell out.

She took them into the conservatory and showed Dad.

He said, "Oh my goodness, this is amazing! This is an old map of Nightingale Square. It is showing a different building, some three hundred years earlier. Look! There are dungeons, and these are tunnels going down to the River Thames."

Mum said, "I don't believe it! And, all the time, they have been here in this house, and New York. I am speechless."

Dad said, "Do you know, it is saying it was an old jailhouse? This could be exactly what we need - I must get back to London asap. Don't tell the kids yet; we don't want to get their hopes up, but this is so exciting."

Meanwhile, Matt and Molly were having a lovely time sledging on their way to Versailles.

They arrived at the entrance to the gardens and Matt got out the codes and clues, and they left their sledge at the gatehouse.

Matt said, "Now, let us go and find this dragon!"

It was easy to walk, as all the paths had been cleared.

Molly said, "It does say the dragon will be kind; I am happy about that."

There were lots of different fountains spraying water up into the air. One had a large, golden-winged monster and, as they got closer, they could see it was a dragon with a plaque saying:

'Dragon fountain of Versailles.'

Molly said, "Well done, Matt, first code. Now let's get going - I'm getting a little cold."

Matt said, "Ask your mate the dragon; after all, he is a fire-eater."

"Very funny," replied Molly.

Matt looked at the next code; it said POOL. He said, "Well, it is not a pool table, not out here."

Molly replied, "The clue said we can see ourselves in it, which means some sort of mirror, or image."

Matt said, "I don't know what kings have got to do with this."

As they walked further, they came across the King's Garden.

Molly said, "Well we have found our KING, so now - a pool we can see ourselves in."

As they walked round, they saw many trees and shrubs, all covered with snow, but still no mirror.

Suddenly, they heard one of the guides telling the visitors, "You don't see a mirror pool every day, a pool fit for a king."

There in front of them, in the middle of the trees, was the King of Versailles - a beautiful mirror-pool.

"Excellent! Another code broken. Now the next one is CHATEAU. That has got to be easy, they are so big," said Matt.

Matt and Molly made their way back to the entrance, as there were toilets and a coffee house, and they also wanted to check that their sledge was still OK.

They were ready for their Coke and piece of cake, and they decided to ask the man in the coffee shop about the chateau.

He only spoke French, and the only word Molly understood was 'petit'. So, off they went, looking for a small chateau.

They walked around the Grand Canal and watched the children playing with their remote-control boats.

Molly said, "That looks fun to do one day; perhaps we should ask Mum and Dad for a boat for Christmas."

They walked all around the gardens then, right at the very end, hidden in the corner, was their petit Trianon, the smallest chateau they had ever seen.

Matt said, "We have done it again! Another code complete. Only one more to go - ORANGES."

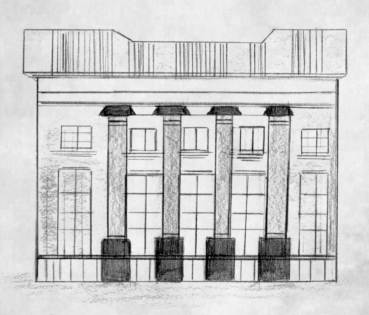

Matt looked at the little map that they had been given at the entrance; they had to make their way back to the front of the gardens.

They noticed a sign saying 'Orangerie'.

Molly said, "It's got to be this way - oranges amongst all the exotic plants."

A gardener looking after the plants heard them and, speaking incredibly good English, said, "No oranges at the moment - it is too cold."

Matt and Molly thanked him and told him his plants were beautiful, even with the snow.

They were both pleased that they had done another good job completing the codes and clues, and they had enjoyed it so much.

When they arrived back home, Mum and Dad were napping in the conservatory.

Then, floating down the stairs, Bertie came to greet them and said, "Hi, you two; how did you get on with the codes and clues?"

Matt replied, "Excellent! We thoroughly enjoyed our morning, and the sledge was brilliant. You know, Bertie, you always use to give us a prize, but Claude does not seem to do that."

Bertie laughed and replied, "Well, ask him what your prize is."

The twins started climbing the stairs, when they heard snoring and, sure enough, behind the airing-cupboard door was Monsieur Claude, fast asleep.

Molly asked, "Why is everyone asleep?"

They all went into Matt's room, and the twins asked Bertie if they could have another look at the map, as now would be the perfect time to talk to Mum and Dad.

Bertie went downstairs to get his cane. When he returned, he unscrewed the top of his cane, but there were no maps to be found.

The Shadow said, "That is strange; the maps were in there yesterday."

Molly said, "Well, where are they?"

"I don't know," he replied. They all decided to go and wake Claude, to see if he had taken another look at them. But no luck.

Molly said, "Well, guys, what are we going to do now? That map was our only chance to save Nightingale Square."

Just then, Mum shouted up the stairs, "Lunch is served, followed by ice cream."

Before they went downstairs Claude asked, "How did you get on with the codes and clues today? You did have a frosty start."

Matt said, "Yes, all done, Claude; do we have a prize for doing such a good job?"

Claude chuckled to himself, put his hand in his shield pocket, and pulled out two ten-euro notes.

"Wow, thank you Claude," they both said.

Mum and Dad were seated at the table, and Dad said, "I am off to London again tomorrow. My company needs some plans for me to look at, and I must take my map over."

Molly whispered to Matt, "He's got it, the map; I know he has it."

After lunch, the twins returned to their room.

The Shadow followed behind and said to Matt,

"That is good news. If you think your Dad has the plans and map, that means you don't have to make up any excuses of how you got them."

"Yes, you're right, Bertie," replied Matt.

Bertie said, "If your Dad can get the jail listed as Grade I, that means we might all be going back home."

Molly said, "Let us hope so."

The next morning, Dad was all packed and ready to go.

Matt, Molly and Mum all said goodbye and wished him luck, and told him to hurry back. Little did Mum know that the twins knew more than her.

Dad was away for nearly a week, and returned to Paris on Friday evening.

Mum gave him a big hug and, before he could get through the door, asked, "How did you do, dear?"

He replied, "Well, I have done all I can; we must keep our fingers crossed - I think Nightingale Square will be saved."

All Matt and Molly dreamt about was going back to Old London Town, to their home in Nightingale Square.

In the morning, the snow had melted, and their little sledge went back up in the roof garden shed.

Even Bertie had a spring in his step, hoping that the old house might be saved from demolition.

There were only two weeks to go before Christmas, and a week left at school.

For Matt and Molly, the week went so slowly. They had so many things to think about - London, school holidays and Cobweb Joe. Would they see him soon?

Can you imagine three ghosts in the house - Bertie, Claude and Cobweb Joe. It does not bear thinking about.

Joyeux Noel

Merry Christmas

From

13 Avenue Silvester de Sacy

Paris

CHAPTER 13

A GHOSTLY ENDING

The London business trip was a success, and Dad had returned just in time for dinner. He told them that Nightingale Square would be protected because they had found an old map and plans that would save it from being demolished.

Matt just winked at Molly. They never said a word.

After supper, the twins went upstairs to complete their homework, which gave Dad a chance to talk to Mum in private.

Mum said, "Do you think there is any chance of us putting in an offer to buy? Is it possible?"

Dad replied, "Don't say anything to Matt and Molly, but I had a chat with my boss, and he said that, because I have travelled a lot over the last few years, they wanted me back in London permanently."

Mum was delighted. "Oh my goodness! The twins are going to be so excited."

Dad said, "That is not the only good news; they have offered me the position of Managing Director, and I would have to start in the New Year. It also comes with a huge bonus, which means we can buy the house, and the company will pay for all our removal costs. How is that for a Christmas present?"

Mum was nearly crying; she could not believe how lucky she felt for her family at that moment. She said, "Well, dear, you definitely deserve something for all your hard work, but this is unbelievable. Well done you." She went and gave him a big hug.

He replied, "No; well done us. You and the kids have always supported me and never moaned about moving; the three of you have been incredible. We all deserve this. Now remember - not a word to the kids."

The following morning, Dad went off to work as usual and, when he returned that evening, he had a big bunch of flowers in his hand.

Molly asked, "What have you done wrong?"

He replied, "Nothing. You will realise when you get older, that little gestures like this count for a lot, just to say 'thank you' and 'I love you'."

Matt laughed and said, "What about me?"

Mum said, "It goes without saying - we love you too."

Mum and Dad went back into the kitchen and the twins went back upstairs. As they reached the top, Monsieur Claude was floating towards them.

"Has the snow disappeared?" he asked.

"Yes," said Matt.

Claude asked the twins, "Would you like to come with me tomorrow to visit the monastery? I have to go and check that everything is in order."

"Oh, yes please," they both replied.

Claude said, "Good. I will enjoy showing you around. Ask Bertie if he would like to join us."

At dinner that evening, they told their parents they were going to visit the old monastery.

Dad said, "That should be interesting; you will enjoy that. I have not seen the old monk at the Tower this evening - he must be at home, counting his money."

The next morning, the twins woke to a cold, crisp, sunny winter's day, perfect for a walk to the old monastery, and the start of a new holiday for Matt and Molly.

Mum had packed them lunch and given them fifteen euros. "I hear the monks make lovely chutney and jams; perhaps you can bring some back with you?"

Just before they walked off down the Avenue, Matt said, "I wonder if Claude has left already? I have not seen him this morning."

Just at that moment, there was a loud clanking noise at the front of the house, and there he was. Claude was sliding down the drainpipe, and his shield was hitting the metal pipe.

"Wait for me," he shouted.

Then Bertie came floating behind. "Don't forget me, guys; I'm coming too."

So off they all trundled. Round the Eiffel Tower and, when they arrived at the Seine, Claude stopped and asked Matt if he would take one of the money bags, as they were rather heavy.

"Of course, give it here," said Matt.

Molly said, "Give me one too, Claude,"

The old monk replied, "Thank you, that is better; a weight off my shoulders."

Eventually, they arrived at the monastery on the outskirts of Paris.

Claude asked, "Well, what do you think of the old place? It is medieval, and has been here for 1,000 years."

Matt, Molly and Bertie followed Claude up to the old oak door. Claude pulled on the rope and the bell above rang out.

The door opened, and there stood another monk, who looked exactly like Monsieur Claude.

"Please, do come in out of the cold," said the old monk.

The twins handed over the money bags and told him that Monsieur Claude had the other one.

"Who is Monsieur Claude?" asked the monk.

Molly replied, "He's one of you."

The monk said, "I do recall we had a Claude here many years ago. Come, let me show you. This book is full of all the monks who have lived here in the last 1,000 years."

He scrolled through from page to page, then the name appeared. "Oh yes, here is Claude. He died in the Hundred Years' War with England, trying to save the monastery from a fire. An exceptionally fine man."

"Yes, we think so," replied Molly.

"Underneath this floor is the crypt where we are all laid to rest. Very peaceful; would you like to look?" asked the old monk.

"Yes, please," said Matt.

Molly was quick to speak: "I'm not sure. I am sure they are very nice - we have met one already. By the way, where are Claude and Bertie?"

The old monk led them down some rickety stairs, and there were old coffins made from marble, with plaques containing all the names of the monks that had been laid to rest.

"Now we are looking for No 13; lucky for some but, unfortunately, not for our friend, Claude."

The old monk finally came across No 13.

"That is strange, the lid has been disturbed and there is a bag of money on the top. Normally, I only get one bag of money per day, but now I have three. Anyway, must get going now, as I have lunch to make. We have fish on the menu today."

He escorted Matt and Molly back to the old entrance door, and thanked them for their pocket money.

Matt and Molly walked back towards the river, wondering where Claude and Bertie were. As they looked back, to their amazement the monastery had disappeared.

Molly said to Matt, "Oh my goodness! Are we dreaming, or is this for real?"

Then Claude and Bertie floated through an old gateway.

"How did you like my monastery?" asked Claude.

Matt replied, "Well, we did find it, but now we have lost it; how come?"

Claude said, "Don't worry; it is still there, but only for people who care."

Matt and Molly were still pinching themselves, as this ghost lark was quite confusing sometimes.

That evening after dinner, Dad said, "Now for the surprise." He fetched the old plans from his briefcase and laid them on the table.

Molly shouted, "You have found them!"

Matt glared at Molly, and nudged her under the table.

Dad said, "Have you seen these before?"

"May have done!" Molly replied.

Dad said, "They fell out of the old cane when Mum was doing the cleaning and, I tell you, they have saved Nightingale Square from demolition."

Matt and Molly both said, "That is good news."

Just at that second there was a *TAP, TAP, TAP.*

Matt and Molly knew **The Shadow** was near, but Dad did not notice. But Mum said, "Now that is spooky. I heard that *TAP, TAP, TAP* when I found the old map; that sent a shiver down my spine."

Molly quickly changed the subject, and asked Dad what would happen next.

Dad said, "Tell me, you two: do you miss our old house in Nightingale Square?"

"Like crazy," said Matt.

Molly said, "We have enjoyed Hong Kong, New York and Paris, but London was our home and we do miss our friends whom we have had since we started school."

Matt asked, "Are we moving back to London?"

Dad replied, "If that is OK with you two."

"It is more than OK," Matt said; he and Molly were jumping around like two-year-olds.

TAP, TAP, TAP

Mum said, "Now, bath and bed for you two; we must start packing tomorrow, as there are only twelve more days till Christmas." They both hugged their parents and could not stop thanking them. Matt said, "This is going to be the best Christmas ever!"

Once they were ready for bed they sat for a while in Matt's room, not quite believing the good news.

Just then, Bertie floated in, and they had never seen him so excited.

Molly said, "Well, Bertie, this means you will be back with your wife."

At that moment, Claude knocked on the balcony door, and Matt went to let him in.

"Hello, you two. Bertie has just told me the good news, but I must say I am really going to miss you all. You have made my life so much fun."

Molly said, "Well, now you have an excuse to come to London and, hopefully, one day you will meet Cobweb Joe. I do believe we have a dungeon and tunnels under the house, so plenty of ghostly things for you and Bertie to get up to."

Molly wrote the London address down, and Claude put it safely into his shield pocket; they all said goodbye. Molly had tears in her eyes.

The next morning was very cold, so Mum made porridge for breakfast. Dad had already left for work, and he had only three more days left.

Mum was extremely busy, spending the next three days packing and cleaning.

Matt said, "We have not heard from Cobweb Joe; we will have to send him our address in London."

Friday came round so quickly, and the family were all packed and ready for their move on Monday morning.

Monday finally arrived, and they had a long drive to Eurotunnel in Calais. The twins had not travelled this way before and thought it was so exciting. It was such fun and, in forty minutes, they were back in England. "Amazing," said Matt.

Molly said, "I was so sad we had to say goodbye to another ghost; first Cobweb Joe, and now Claude. I do hope that, one day, they come to visit."

Dad told Matt and Molly that they were going to their grandparents, as the old house would not be ready to move in until New Year.

"Can we still go and see it before then?" asked Matt.

"Of course," replied Dad.

It was a long drive back, and Nana and Grandad were so pleased to see them. They were overjoyed that, this time, it was for good.

Grandad said, "Now, you have not brought any ghosts with you, I hope?"

Matt and Molly went up to their rooms and opened the balcony door.

Matt said, "Oh, Molly, we are so lucky to be back home. Look! Over on the Thames, Tower Bridge is up and letting a boat through; that is so good to see. Now that is a good homecoming!"

"I'm with you on that one," replied Molly.

Grandad said, "We have booked a table tonight for dinner, our treat. It is the one you and Molly like, Matt; the other side of Tower Bridge."

Matt said, "Great! It is *The Shadow*'s favourite place."

"Who is *The Shadow*?" Grandad replied.

Mum muttered, "It's all in their minds, Dad; it is a ghost with a hat and cane."

Dad said, "What did you just say? Hat and cane?"

"Yes, but where are they?" asked Mum.

Dad replied, "In Paris. I left them on the stand, as you are always saying they are fit for the bin."

Matt and Molly went upstairs to change for dinner.

Molly said, "We have left Bertie there; how stupid are we? We were so busy sorting ourselves out - now he's with Claude in Paris. What a mess!"

At that moment, Grandad shouted upstairs, "Come on, you two! The Italian is calling."

When they left the restaurant, it was snowing heavily and there were already three inches on the ground.

Molly said, "Perfect, just in time for Christmas."

The family had a lovely evening discussing what they were going to do first. I do not know who was more excited, Nan and Grandad for having them back safe, Matt and Molly because it had been their dream, or Mum and Dad, who finally felt settled.

The next morning, Dad had to talk with the builders, and was so pleased, as they said they would be in for Christmas Eve and they would return to complete the work on the dungeons and tunnels after the Christmas holidays.

Dad said, "Yes, and thank goodness we have got the house listed Grade I, so we were able to get a grant; and to think it was down to that old hat and cane, and the map we found!"

Mum said, "Excellent! Now we can go and get the biggest Christmas tree ever."

Christmas Eve arrived so fast. With all the decorations going up and the snow still falling, it was magical.

Matt and Molly were up in their old rooms, and Molly said, "I do hope the builders did not frighten Bertie's wife away." Then, just at that moment, there was an enormous thud coming from the attic.

They both jumped up and ran upstairs and there, in the middle of the floor, was *The Shadow*'s little, leather-bound book.

Matt said, "That is strange. I thought Bertie still had it with him." There was a page sticking out; it said:

'HAPPY NEW YEAR'
We will all give out a big cheer

Matt and Molly looked at each other, and Matt said, "He will be here, by New Year's Eve."

I think they both knew in their hearts he would be there - it was a sign!

They went back downstairs, and Mum said, "Look! The old hat stand is still here; we must keep it. After all, it is part of the furniture."

Dad said, "The lorry will be here soon, with all our bits and pieces."

Mum said, "I think a New Year's shopping spree is on the cards."

Once the furniture arrived, Mum delegated a place for each piece, and the removal men did a grand job with Mum's guidance.

Matt and Molly, and their family, could not have asked for a better Christmas - it was fab.

Mum and Dad sent out cards and phoned friends, inviting them all to a New Year's party, fancy dress with a ghostly feel, of course.

They decorated the house ready for a party to remember, with a little help from Matt and Molly.

New Year's Eve, and it was party time. Big Ben rang out 9 chimes and Mum said, "Only three hours to go till countdown."

All their friends had turned up, and Matt and Molly had invited a few of their old friends who they went to school with. They played party games while the parents were chatting and celebrating their return.

Mum announced, "Only ten minutes till midnight. There are fireworks over Tower Bridge - let us go into the Square to toast in the New Year."

Big Ben struck midnight, and fireworks flashed out over the Thames, with lights flashing, champagne corks popping and streamers falling.

Then suddenly, out of the mist with lights flashing, was an old, open-top double-decker *Routemaster* bus. The twins gasped as it turned into the Square.

As if their Christmas and New Year could not get any better, there, right in front of their eyes, were their old friends, Bertie, Cobweb Joe and Claude.

Cobweb Joe was in the cab, driving the bus. Bertie was acting as a ticket inspector, hanging from the pole, while Claude was on the top deck, dancing in front of two loudspeakers.

Matt and Molly ran over to them, "Guys! What a lovely surprise! Where have you been?"

Joe replied, "We are all staying at Clink Jail, waiting for our new home, Nightingale Dungeons, to be renovated; but tonight, it is:

PARTY TIME, 'HIT IT CLAUDE'

The music started playing, and Mum shouted to Dad, "It is our song!" and everybody started dancing to *The Monster Mash* - it caught on in a flash. Mum said, "Look dear, at those people on the bus - they look brilliant in fancy dress!"

What a New Year to remember: Dad, the new Managing Director, Mum's new book, and Matt and Molly's dream that came true. And do not let us forget our

'FOUR NEW TENANTS'

THE END

Matt and Molly's adventures happened far and wide
Do come along just for the ride

London, New York, and Paris City
This is the end, oh what a pity

With all the codes and clues on the way
With Bertie, Joe and Claude having their say

Matt and Molly have learnt so much
Keep reading their books and keep in touch

Their mate *The Shadow* and wife are clever
Made a home in the basement now and forever

Mum and Dad don't know half that's gone on
Only that the hat and cane have finally gone

Matt and Molly have their lives ahead
Plenty more books are in their head

Ghosts will appear now and again
When Bertie comes calling and tapping his cane

Goodbye my friends, Au revoir for now
Love ya, dudes, we are taking a bow

Loykey & Lillybit

The Shadow of Old London Town

The Shadow of Old London Town
A BITE OUT OF THE BIG APPLE

The Shadow of Old London Town
AN EYEFUL OF THE TOWER

****

Alice and Alfie and the magic windmill

Alice and Alfie and the magic windmill
THE RETURN OF NICHOLE

Alice and Alfie and the magic windmill
BEST FRIENDS